SURVIVAL TAILS

THE TITANIC

SURVIVAL TAILS

THE TITANIC
Book 1

By Katrina Charman

LITTLE, BROWN AND COMPANY
NEW YORK BOSTON

Copyright © 2018 by Katrina Charman
Interior art © 2018 by Owen Richardson

Cover art copyright © 2018 by Owen Richardson. Cover design by Nicole Brown.
Cover copyright © 2018 by Hachette Book Group, Inc.

Little, Brown and Company
Hachette Book Group
1290 Avenue of the Americas, New York, NY 10104
Visit us at LBYR.com

First Edition: March 2018

Little, Brown and Company is a division of Hachette Book Group, Inc.
The Little, Brown name and logo are trademarks of Hachette Book Group, Inc.

The publisher is not responsible for websites (or their content)
that are not owned by the publisher.

Library of Congress Cataloging-in-Publication Data
Names: Charman, Katrina, author.
Title: The Titanic / by Katrina Charman.
Description: First edition. | New York : Little, Brown and Company, 2018. | Series: Survival
tails ; book 1 | Summary: "A stowaway dog and the captain's cat forge an unlikely friendship
as they race to protect three kittens, help their humans, and survive the sinking of the Titanic."
Identifiers: LCCN 2017027420| ISBN 9780316477857 (hardcover) | ISBN 9780316477833
(trade pbk.) | ISBN 9780316477826 (ebook) | ISBN 9780316477840 (library ebook edition)
Subjects: LCSH: Titanic (Steamship)—Juvenile fiction. | CYAC: Titanic (Steamship)—Fiction. |
Survival—Fiction. | Shipwrecks—Fiction. | Dogs—Fiction. | Cats—Fiction. | Animals—
Infancy—Fiction. | Stowaways—Fiction.
Classification: LCC PZ7.1.C495 Tit 2018 | DDC [Fic]—dc23
LC record available at https://lccn.loc.gov/2017027420

ISBNs: 978-0-316-47785-7 (hardcover), 978-0-316-47783-3 (pbk.),
978-0-316-47782-6 (ebook)

Printed in the United States of America

LSC-C

10 9 8 7 6 5 4 3 2 1

For Maddie, Piper, and Riley.
And Gemma, for everything.

CHAPTER 1
MUTT

Tuesday, April 9, 1912

The rain fell softly, swirling around the small garden to land on Mutt's wiry, dull brown fur. It was the kind of rain that seemed barely there at all when you looked out from the dry comfort of indoors—little more than a mist on the wind. But when you had no choice but to be out in it, it was almost as wet as a full-pelt downpour.

Mutt looked around the garden for some kind of shelter. There was a small vegetable patch with sprouting potato plants, carrots, and radishes, and a wooden outhouse that leaned against the back of the house, but the master kept that locked. Mutt sneezed, covering his head with his paws, but the rain continued to *drip drip drip* into his eyes no matter what he did.

Mutt hated getting wet.

He hated being in trouble even more, though. The master had caught him earlier that day trying to dig up some radishes and, after a loud telling-off, had tied Mutt to the rickety garden fence. The master was a fisherman by trade and knew how to tie an unyielding knot better than anyone.

Mutt tried once more to wriggle his way free from the old, fraying rope, which smelled like seaweed and mackerel, but despite his tugging, and gnawing, and squirming, the knot held fast. Now the sky was darkening, his teeth were sore, and his neck throbbed with a painful heat beneath the rope. The worst part of all was that if the master was angry with Mutt, he would be angry with Alice, too.

Mutt was going nowhere.

His stomach growled and he let out a small whine to get the master's attention in case he had forgotten that Mutt was there. Inside the house Mutt saw the looming shadow of the master lit by the dim, flickering lamplight, but nobody came to the door. Mutt caught the scent of something rich and delicious, and his stomach growled again. He imagined that they might have lit the fire; the night was cold enough for it, even though it was early April and flowers were sprouting up all over the village.

Finally, the rain eased off, and the back door slammed open suddenly, followed by a booming yell.

"Alice!"

Alice ran outside, bright red hair streaking behind her as her bare feet slapped across the wet mud. She threw herself down beside Mutt and buried her face in his fur, not caring that it was filthy and stinking and wet. He nuzzled into her neck, feeling all the warmer for having her close by. There was no better feeling on earth, Mutt thought, than being with his girl. He sniffed and licked at Alice's hands to see if she'd brought him anything to eat, but they were empty.

"Alice! Get back here now," the master roared from the doorway.

Mutt froze, his ears flattening against his head and his tail dropping between his legs as he shrank backward. Alice clung to Mutt tighter than the rope around his neck.

"I won't leave him!" Alice wailed, pulling Mutt closer.

The master gave a loud grunt and yanked on his

boots, then sloshed toward them. Mutt chanced a quick glance, but instead of finding the usual wrinkled brow and scowl, he saw that the master seemed almost sad.

"Alice," the master said again, his gruff voice quieter. "We can't take him with us."

"Why not?" Alice asked, the sound muffled by Mutt's overgrown fur.

"Because we can't. Dogs aren't allowed on the big steamers," the master replied, crouching beside Alice.

Mutt's ears pricked up. Alice had been out fishing plenty of times on the master's lugger, but never on a steamer. The steamers were the biggest of all the ships... like entire floating villages. Mutt cocked his head to one side, an uneasy feeling growing in his stomach that had nothing to do with his hunger; humans only went on a steamer when they were going somewhere far, far away.

The master put his large, callused hand on Alice's shoulder, but she shrugged him off.

"Other people take their dogs on boats!" she cried, wiping the tears across her face with her nightdress's sleeve. Mutt licked at her tears, but the master gave him a sharp look and he slunk back again.

"Mary Parker told me so," Alice continued. "Her

cousin, Alfie, works down at the shipyard. He's seen plenty of people take animals onto the big ships. Not just dogs, neither—live chickens, and pigs, and even big colorful birds in wire cages."

The master rubbed a hand over his face and sighed. "Not people like us, though."

He pulled a folded piece of paper out of his jacket pocket and opened it to show Alice. In the darkness, it was too difficult to read the writing printed on it, but Mutt could just about make out a small design at the top of the paper—a red flag with a white star in the middle.

"We're in steerage," the master said. "Third class. We're lucky they let poor people like *us* on such a fine ship, let alone an old mutt." He jerked his head toward Mutt and let out a small huff of a laugh. "Besides, he's too chickenhearted to set foot on my old lugger, let alone the biggest ship in the world."

Mutt gave a gruff bark in protest, but the master ignored him.

"It's not his fault he doesn't like water," Alice said, kissing Mutt's head in sympathy. She glanced at the paper in her father's hand, curiosity getting the better of her. "Is it *really* the biggest ship in the world?"

The master nodded. "Just think of it, Alice. It'll be a new life for us...a new world. And we'll be traveling there on the most luxurious ship that was ever built."

Alice leaned forward to get a closer look. "The *Titanic*," she whispered.

Mutt whined as she pulled away from him. He yanked at the rope, but it tightened around his throat with each tug. When it became almost too tight to bear, he changed tack, scratching and digging at the sodden ground to loosen the fence post. He wouldn't let Alice leave without him. He couldn't.

"Mutt, you'll hurt yourself!" Alice cried, loosening the rope slightly and stroking his head. She scratched him in his favorite spot beneath his chin and he calmed a little. Of course she wouldn't let the master leave him behind. She would find a way to persuade her father—she always did. After all, Mutt belonged to Alice. Alice belonged to Mutt. It was the way it had always been.

"He knows something's wrong," Alice told her father, her eyes brimming with tears again. "Can't we at least bring him inside? His fur is soaked through."

The master glanced at Mutt and paused. "It's best if he stays out here for now," he said.

Alice rested her face against Mutt's and he licked at her cheek again. It tasted like sea salt and blackberries. "But he's my best friend," Alice said quietly. "Mam would have let me."

If the master heard, he made no reply. The three of them sat silently, surrounded by the familiar sounds of distant gulls and the echo of foghorns.

"Your mam would have wanted us to take this opportunity," the master said finally. "Now, come along inside; you'll catch a chill."

"Who will look after Mutt?" Alice asked.

"Peter Craggs is coming by in the morning to collect him," the master said. "It's all been arranged."

"Peter Craggs!" Alice shrieked. "Mutt hates Peter Craggs, and Peter Craggs hates Mutt. He told me so himself."

Mutt growled in agreement. Peter Craggs smelled worse than fish guts on a hot day. The boy had thrown pebbles at him and Alice last week when they were scavenging along the beach. She and Mutt had chased the boy all the way back to the village green.

The master huffed. "No one else will take him, Alice. He's not the best-behaved dog."

"Oh, Papa, *please!*" Alice begged. "Mutt is family! We could hide him in our trunk...or we could stay here....I don't want to go to the New World. Let's stay here. Please, Papa!"

"They'd throw Mutt overboard if they discovered him, and then they'd send us right back home." The master shook his head. "The ship leaves tomorrow at noon and we're going to be on it."

Alice pulled Mutt closer than ever, crying huge, wrenching sobs that vibrated through Mutt's entire body.

Mutt yowled, his own lament rising above Alice's until he couldn't hear her crying anymore. It grew louder still when the master yelled at him to shut up before old Mrs. Walton came knocking. But Mutt yowled loudest of all when the master pulled Alice away and dragged her inside the house, bolting the door.

Leaving Mutt tied to the rickety fence, alone in the cold, wet garden.

CHAPTER 2
MUTT

Wednesday, April 10, 1912

Mutt had lived by the sea his whole life—or at least for as long as he could remember. On sunny days he and Alice would scour the beach in Southampton. Mutt made sure not to venture too close to the water as they searched for treasure among the flotsam and jetsam that washed up on the river's edge, dragged in from the Solent. Mutt himself had been one of Alice's grander finds: a newborn pup, tangled up among some old fishing nets and huddled beneath the seaweed.

Once, they'd found a rocking chair, surprisingly intact but in need of a good cleanup. Alice had somehow managed to drag it along the shingle beach and all the way home. Her mother reckoned that it came from a wrecked pirate ship and had probably belonged to the pirate captain himself. The master had snorted at that, saying that no pirate worth his salt would be caught dead in a grimy old rocking chair.

But Alice's mother wanted to keep it, so she helped Alice clean it up and sand it down and give it a bit of a polish. When they'd finished, it looked as good as new. Alice's mother had spent many a night rocking beside the fire while she spun tales. Then she'd caught the sickness, but sat there still, with the master fussing while Alice sat beside her, and Mutt on top of Mam's feet. Until one morning, it was just the three of them...and the empty rocking chair.

Mutt woke from his sleep with a start, his tail numb. He thought he'd heard Alice calling, but when he looked over at the house, all was quiet. The sun had only just started to rise—a pale orange smear on the horizon. The master was usually out on his lugger before dawn for the best catch. But he wouldn't be going out on his lugger today. Nor any day after.

Mutt scratched at the sodden ground, no longer

caring about wet paws. He chewed at the rope at the same time, doubling his efforts. His tongue hung from his mouth as he panted, digging harder, faster. He *had* to get to Alice before she was gone for good. With a final, determined burst of energy, he pulled hard and the rotting post gave way slightly. Encouraged, Mutt pulled harder, the rope burning at his skin, until finally the post tore free from the ground, sending Mutt flying backward into a puddle. He gripped the rope with his teeth, easing the end up and over the wooden post.

He was free!

Mutt pawed at the rope around his neck until it slipped to the ground. With his damp fur warmed by the sun, he shook his body in triumph, sending mud flying everywhere. He trotted over to the house, sniffing at the small gap beneath the back door.

There were no sounds. No smells. No Alice! Mutt's stomach lurched as he realized they must already have left. The sun was higher now and the master had said that the boat sailed at noon. The boy—Peter—would be coming for Mutt soon. He *had* to get to the docks.

Mutt raced down to the shore, his claws scrabbling across the loose pebbles as he ran. He'd seen the big ships coming in and out of the big blue enough times to know where they sailed from. All he had to do was follow the shoreline until he found Alice's steamer. He headed farther inland, glancing across the river to the docks in the distance, then paused. The boats sailed from the *opposite* side of the water. He'd have to follow the river all the way to the bridge to reach Alice's ship, which would mean half a day's journey at least. Or he could take the nearby floating bridge, which meant going *over* the water.

The floating bridge was like a barge—made from wood and powered by steam. It was linked to heavy chains laid across the riverbed that reeled the bridge back and forth, back and forth, a thousand times a day. It was the only way to get across the water without swimming, and the easiest and quickest way to get to Alice's ship in time.

As Mutt reached the bridge and crept closer to the water's edge, his hackles rose. His stomach told him to *stay back! Don't go any closer!* but he swallowed his fear and pushed forward, stepping onto the barge with trembling paws.

There was a sudden jolt as the bridge began to move.

The rumble of chains vibrated through the wooden planks beneath Mutt's paws and he dug his claws in, squeezing his eyes shut. He tried to still his shaky legs and calm his racing heart. Most of all, he tried not to think of the sloshing water surrounding the barge, or what might happen if he fell overboard.

After a few agonizing minutes, they reached the opposite bank. As soon as the bridge was close to the shore, Mutt raced to disembark, stumbling because his legs were still wobbly.

Relief flooded through him as he set his paws onto the heavenly solid ground. He had paused for a moment to get his bearings when he noticed a poster pasted on the wall in front of him. At the top was the same design he had seen on the master's ticket—a red flag with a white star—above a picture of a huge ship. Below that, in bright, bold letters, the words *The Ship of Dreams*.

Mutt raced to the end of the street, following the ever-increasing noise and the flow of humans, carts, and carriages laden with suitcases and trunks. He turned the next corner and stopped dead. In front of him, taller than any building he'd ever seen and as long as any street, was the ship—the *Titanic*. Towering high above him, four colossal cream-colored funnels topped with black reached to the sky.

All around, humans bustled: loading the ship with crates and passengers' belongings; saying goodbyes; admiring the breathtaking sight of the world's biggest ship. Mutt wove his way through the crowd, around legs and trunks and crates, sniffing the air for Alice's scent. At one point he thought he saw a flash of her red hair, but it was lost in the throng.

"Third class, this way!" a voice yelled above the commotion.

Mutt's ears pricked up. The master had told Alice that they were traveling in third class!

He followed the voice to where a line of humans waited at the end of a long walkway. It led from the quayside to an open door at the lower part of the ship. Many of the third-class passengers had only one bag. Others had nothing but the clothes on their back and a piece of paper in their hand—their ticket to a new life. A world away from the vast trunks and packages that the first-class passengers had.

At the front of the line, a man in a black uniform and hat carried out checks of the third-class passengers' hair, eyes, and teeth. One by one, the humans stepped up to be examined before being allowed on board. It reminded Mutt of the way Alice sometimes checked his fur for fleas, and he wondered if the humans were doing the same thing.

Mutt sneaked alongside the line, glad he couldn't see the water. He paused, taking a deep breath as he steeled himself to step onto the steamer. Telling himself over and over that he could do it. He *could* get on the boat. He *could* go onto the water. He *would* do it.

For Alice.

He would cross the big blue a thousand times over if it meant he would be with his girl.

Mutt continued on, hiding behind a large lady who had a particularly wide, long skirt that bloomed around her legs like a flower. As she moved, so did Mutt. He darted behind her skirt, keeping low to the ground and as close to the woman as he dared. She reached the front of the line to be checked over and Mutt stayed as still as he could, barely daring to breathe.

"Go ahead," the man said.

Mutt peeped out from the hem of the skirt at the same time that the man checked his pocket watch, catching Mutt's eye. He frowned, then held out his arm, stopping the lady in her tracks.

"No dogs allowed," he grunted, nodding at Mutt.

The woman blinked, then let out an ear-piercing shriek as Mutt peered sheepishly back up at her. She swung her handbag, hitting Mutt full-force in the head before he had a chance to scarper. With a low whine, Mutt turned and ran as fast as he could, back down the walkway, the woman's high-pitched squeals echoing after him as he hid among the bales, sacks, and barrels on the quayside.

There *had* to be another way onto the ship. It would be sailing soon, and it couldn't leave without him. He had to get to Alice. Mutt glanced around desperately, his head throbbing and his body shaking as he took a peek at the walkway again. The uniformed man's back was turned, and Mutt seized his chance. There was no more time to think, or worry, or plan. He couldn't give up now, not when he was so close. He bolted between the legs of two humans, swerving around a small boy who tried to grab his tail as he passed, heading full-pelt toward the door.

Almost there, almost made it, Mutt was thinking, when out of nowhere a burly docker with a very large, pointy hook stepped right into his path. Mutt barely managed to come to a stop before turning tail and retreating to his hiding place among the crates, not sure that he had the strength or nerve left in him for another attempt. He lay on the ground panting, frantically trying to think of another way onto the ship.

"That didn't go too well, did it?" a small voice said with a snicker.

Mutt almost jumped out of his fur. He spun around, startled, to see who or what had spoken.

"If you want to get on that ship, you've got to be a bit smarter than that," the voice said.

"Who's there?" Mutt barked.

A sharp, tangy smell hit his nose, along with something more familiar—the earthy scent of freshly dug vegetables packed into one of the crates nearby. Beneath that was something that made Mutt's stomach churn— the dank, rotten smell that came with sickness and disease and dead things.

Rats.

"Up here," the voice said.

Mutt bared his teeth, looking up to see two beady black eyes peering back at him from atop the crate.

"I suppose," the rat said, "I could help you."

"I don't need your help," Mutt growled.

"Is that so?" the rat replied, raising his eyebrows. "Well then, if you don't want my advice, try your way again. See how far you get."

Mutt glanced up at the rat, then back at the ship. The burly man patrolled up and down in front of the walkway, swinging his hook in the air with an audible *swoosh*.

"See, your *first* mistake was trying to get on the ship with the *humans*," the rat said. "You are not a human. And unless you're one of those well-to-do pampered pets"—he looked Mutt over and crinkled his nose—"which you *obviously* are not, then you have no chance."

"What would a stinking rat know about it?" Mutt snarled, ducking low as a dark shadow passed over them.

"Oh, not much, I suppose," the rat snickered. "I've only traveled on ships *hundreds* of times. I was born at sea on a pirate ship, one dark and stormy night, somewhere in the middle of the Caribbean, so the story goes. But—if you don't want my help..."

The rat shrugged, jumping down from the crate with a thud to scurry off toward the ship. He was bigger than most rats Mutt had encountered and had a red crusty-looking stump where his tail should have been.

"Wait!" Mutt barked.

The rat turned slowly, gesturing to himself with a paw. "Who, me? A stinking old rat?"

Mutt held back the growl building in his throat. Every part of him wanted to pounce on the rat and rip him to pieces, but he needed to get onto that ship. And if a rat could help him do that, he couldn't be fussy. "Yes, you."

The rat grinned. "I'll help you…if you say please."

"Just tell me how to get onto the ship," Mutt snapped. "I need to find my human."

The rat scuttled closer, cocking his head to one side. "Your human?"

Mutt nodded. "She's on that ship."

"Are you sure she wants you to find her? After all, if she wanted you with her, she would have taken you— like that one there."

He jerked his nose toward a well-dressed lady who was carrying the most ridiculous-looking dog Mutt had ever seen. It had fluffed-up white fur and a pink bow around its neck. Mutt's lip curled. Dogs like that gave his kind a bad name.

"She would have taken me if she could, but she's in

third class. It's not allowed," Mutt explained. He paced back and forth, getting more and more desperate by the second as he watched the final passengers board. He paused as a thought occurred to him. "Why do you want to help me?"

The rat winked. "I might ask you to repay the favor sometime."

Mutt narrowed his eyes at the rat, but he didn't have many other options. "Fine." He sighed, wondering what kind of favor a rat could possibly ask for.

The rat gave Mutt a sly, toothy grin. "How do you feel about small, dark spaces?"

CHAPTER 3

CLARA

Wednesday, April 10, 1912

Clara despised being kept in a basket. It was so undignified. The captain knew perfectly well that she could sit beside him in the motorcar without having to be imprisoned.

But the driver had insisted when he'd picked them up from their manor house. He didn't want the cat to "soil the interior," he said. So with an apologetic look and a stroke of her head, the captain had reluctantly agreed and placed Clara inside a wicker basket.

"Is this really necessary?" the captain asked the driver as they traveled to the docks, reaching his fingers in to stroke Clara's face.

"Sorry, sir," the driver replied. "The boss will have my guts for garters if anything gets on the upholstery."

Clara turned her nose up at the driver, even though he couldn't see her. The car bumped over a series of deep potholes along the dirt road and she shrieked, swallowing down the urge to regurgitate her breakfast of pilchards and goat's milk. Although, she thought, maybe she would do it anyway to teach the rotten driver a lesson.

Clara couldn't wait to be back on a ship, with the wind in her fur and miles of ocean stretching around them as they sailed smoothly across the waves—free of the endless bumps and jolts she was enduring in the motorcar.

"I really must insist," the captain said as Clara screeched again.

He ignored the driver's protests, lifting Clara out of the basket and onto his lap, stroking her head to calm her. "If there is any damage at all," the captain told the driver, "I will pay for it."

That seemed to satisfy the driver well enough, and Clara licked at her paws in victory, purring as loudly as she could to irritate the driver. The captain chuckled and kissed her on the head.

"I've never heard of a captain having a cat before," the driver said as they pulled up at the docks where their ship was waiting.

"She is a very special cat," the captain said. "She has accompanied me on many voyages over the years. I would be lost without her."

The captain stepped out of the car, carrying Clara in his arms. The driver unloaded their things. Clara felt a shiver of excitement as she took in the magnificent sight of what would be her home for the next few weeks. They would sail from Southampton to New York and back home again, making stops at Cherbourg in France and Queenstown in Ireland to pick up and offload more passengers and mail.

Setting her down on the ground, Clara's captain stood beside her for a moment, observing the crowd. Clara herself stared up in awe at the magnificent ship.

Of all the ships Clara had sailed on—and there had been many—the *Titanic* was by far the finest. The unsinkable ship! That was what the humans were calling it. And indeed it did seem that a ship so well built and luxurious could be immortal.

Some of the world's richest and most famous humans

would be joining the *Titanic*'s maiden voyage, including the multimillionaire John Jacob Astor IV, and Isidor Straus, owner of Macy's department store, and his wife, Ida. Even the ship's architect, Thomas Andrews, and the chairman of the White Star Line, J. Bruce Ismay, would be on board, making sure that everything went smoothly and taking notes on anything that needed altering. Although Clara couldn't see what could possibly need changing. The *Titanic* was flawless (aside from a half-eaten sandwich inside the Turkish baths she'd found when accompanying the captain on his inspection, and that would be long gone by now).

Clara looked up at the captain, and when he smiled back at her she couldn't help but feel a burst of pride. As they walked toward the gangplank, they were stopped several times by first-class passengers wanting to greet the captain and shake his hand. Clara made sure to stay a few steps behind; the passengers wanted to speak to the famous Captain Edward John Smith, not pet his cat.

"Captain Smith!" a finely dressed woman trilled, hurrying over to lay a gloved hand on the captain's sleeve while she juggled a tiny dog beneath her arm. "So lovely to see you again!" she gushed. "Of course I insisted on sailing on the *Titanic* as soon as I heard you were to be her captain."

The captain smiled and nodded politely at the woman, then moved along to the next person wanting his attention.

The officers paid Clara no mind as she followed the captain to the gangplank, where they were lined up waiting for the captain to board. He greeted them in turn, and only one of the younger officers, who Clara had never met before, glanced down at her, giving her a bemused look as she trotted along behind her captain, with her nose in the air and her tail held high.

The ship's trio of tall bronze whistles sounded, and Clara again felt the flutter of excitement in her stomach. The feeling that she was exactly where she belonged. That she was home.

CHAPTER 4
MUTT

Wednesday, April 10, 1912
Noon

Mutt stared into one of what seemed like hundreds of huge sacks full of letters and parcels piled up on the quayside ready to be loaded onto the ship. "You want me to get into that?" he asked the rat, who was chewing at the rope tied around one of the mail sacks. "That's your grand plan?"

His heart raced just thinking about it. How was he going to breathe? What if the sack he was in fell into the water? What if he became trapped? He hated sacks almost as much as he hated water, and now here he was, having to confront both of his worst fears.

"It's your best way onto the ship," the rat told him. "Unless you want to squeeze that big head of yours into the gap in one of those crates?"

Mutt glanced over at the crates filled with fruits and vegetables that were being hoisted one by one by large cranes into the cargo hold of the ship. He would never fit.

"Is that how you get on board?"

The rat nodded. "Only the best for us rats. There's enough food in there to keep us going just in case...." He caught the anxious expression on Mutt's face and waved a paw at him. "Relax! I've been on these ships a thousand times. Nothing's ever gone wrong before. And just wait till you see the food the humans eat! The last trip I took, I was double the size by the time we docked."

Mutt could believe it. He wasn't a small dog, and the rat was almost half his size.

"The name's Leon, by the way," the rat said, holding out a paw. "King Leon."

Mutt ignored the paw and narrowed his eyes, suspicious once again. He had never heard of such a thing as a royal rat. "King?"

"That's right." King Leon nodded, standing up on his back legs so that he was almost nose to nose with

Mutt. He placed his paws on his hips. "You, my friend, are in the presence of rat royalty. King Leon the Three Hundred and Thirty-Third—give or take a few—descended from the great rat king of Brooklyn himself." He dropped back down on all fours and gave a little shrug. "Well, me and about a billion other rats."

"You're from Brooklyn?" Mutt asked, realizing why the rat spoke in an unfamiliar accent. "Is that in the New World? What's it like?"

"The New World?" King Leon said. "I don't know much about it being the New World, but it's as good a world as any."

The air vibrated with a sudden, deafening whistle and the crowd of humans lining the quayside started to wave and cheer.

King Leon gestured to the sack beside them. "Hop inside and try to make yourself as small as possible—and keep that wagging tail of yours still."

As much as Mutt hated the idea of climbing into a sack, the thought of never seeing Alice again was worse. He swallowed the last of his fear and jumped into the mail sack, wriggling and squirming his way down among the brown-paper-covered parcels and bundles of letters until he was covered well enough so that none of the humans would notice him.

The minutes ticked painfully by. Mutt considered whether he should trust the rat and stay put, or find another way on board. As far as he could tell, the rat— *King Leon*—had long since disappeared. Mutt wondered if he would see him again, although he didn't much care either way. The last thing he needed was to owe a *rat* a favor.

All of a sudden, the sack shifted and Mutt felt it being lifted off the ground. Through a gap that opened up at the mouth of the sack, he saw the hull of the big ship. Huge, towering white letters painted on the side read TITANIC.

This was it! His belly swirled with a mixture of fear and anticipation. He couldn't wait to see the look on Alice's face when they were reunited. The master might be a little less pleased, but Mutt was sure he'd get used to the idea. Besides, he *was* always complaining that Mutt should go on a boat to get over his fear of water, and it wasn't as if he'd actually let anyone throw Mutt overboard.

Finally, the swaying movement stopped and everything went dark. King Leon had told him to lie low until the ship got moving, but Mutt felt too anxious. He thought of Alice and how her face lit up whenever she saw him, and it calmed him a little. As the minutes turned to hours, it didn't seem as if they had moved at all. It was too hot and too dark, and Mutt was starting to panic that he might never get out. Not to mention the fact that his rump was numb and no matter how many times he changed position, there was always something with a pointy edge digging into him.

Mutt had a sudden horrifying thought—what if Alice *had* managed to change the master's mind? What if, at that very moment, they were at home while Mutt was heading out into the big blue? What would Alice do when she found Mutt gone?

He wriggled his way through the parcels and letters piled on top of him, bursting from the top of the sack and sending the mail flying out with him. Then he clambered over the mountain of sacks identical to his own, searching for a door or a way out of the storage compartment, which was lit by a single lightbulb. But all he found was a metal door that seemed to be locked from the outside.

Mutt whined, scratching against the metal. He was

trapped. He would starve to death and Alice would never know that he had tried to find her. He scratched and scratched at the door until his paws ached. Eventually hunger and exhaustion caught up with him and he crumpled onto a sack of mail destined for a world he'd likely never see.

CHAPTER 5

CLARA

Thursday, April 11, 1912

Clara followed the captain out of the wheelhouse and past his sleeping quarters, prowling along the first-class promenade toward the stern as her master made his daily routine checks. Clara heard the captain telling some of the passengers that they might make it to America in less than seven days with the engines at full speed and if the weather was good. Clara wasn't as worried about reaching their destination quickly. She was just glad to have the chance to accompany her captain on his final voyage before he retired, and she, as captain's cat, with him.

Clara continued along the boat deck. She padded

silently past the lifeboats that lined the uppermost deck, past the Marconi room, where the wireless operators communicated with nearby ships and with the shore when they were close enough. She passed by the magnificent, ornate dome of glass that topped the grand staircase, then a curious room filled with equipment that the humans used for exercise. Then on to the second-class promenade toward the stern of the ship, and past the first-class smoking room.

There were more lifeboats at the back of the ship. As Clara approached, she heard a strange sound coming from the one farthest away. She sneaked over and listened, her ears pricked up. A small squeak came from inside the boat, followed by another. Clara slunk low to the floor, her claws out as she prowled closer, thinking that a rat would make a satisfying meal. She pounced up onto the canvas lifeboat cover, easing her head beneath the rim. But she didn't find rats. To her surprise, three black-and-white kittens huddled beneath one of the wooden benches, mewing for their mother.

Clara squeezed her body beneath the tight gap between the canvas cover and the edge of the boat and sniffed at the kittens. "How did you get inside here?"

she asked the largest of the kittens, who stared up at her with wide blue eyes.

"Our mother left us here," the kitten replied.

"Your mother?" Clara sniffed the air.

The kitten nodded. "She said she would come back, but that was a very long time ago."

Another of the kittens gave a small cry. "Where's our mother? We're so hungry."

Clara couldn't answer. She didn't understand how the kittens could have been left inside a lifeboat in the first place. The only thing she knew for sure was that there were no other cats on the ship besides her and these three little stowaways.

"Did your mother name you?" she asked the kittens.

The largest kitten nodded. "I'm Violet," she said. "These are my brothers—Cosmo and Jack."

Clara looked at each of the kittens in turn, trying to decide what she should do. If she left them there, they would likely starve before they reached their destination. But if she helped them, she might never shake them. Kittens had a nasty habit of becoming attached.

"You may call me Miss Clara," she said finally. "I am the captain's cat."

Jack's eyes widened at this. Apparently feeling a little bit brave, he ventured forward, standing as tall as he could to raise his small pink nose to Clara. "Will you help us find our mother, Miss Clara?" he asked.

"You can't stay here," Clara told him, ignoring his question. "If humans find you, they will throw you overboard."

Cosmo squeaked, and Violet narrowed her eyes at Clara, licking Cosmo's head to calm him. Jack, pretending not to have heard her last remark, said, "You could look after us. Until our mother returns."

Clara frowned and shook her head. She had far more important things to be doing than looking after abandoned kittens. Clara had never had kittens herself— she'd always been too busy traveling on ships with her captain. She'd never once regretted it, and she wasn't about to spend her final years chasing kittens around.

"You'll have to fend for yourselves," she told the kittens, making a decision. "Though if you don't want to be discovered or starve before we reach land, you'll need to find a safer place to hide."

"Where can we go?" Cosmo squeaked.

Clara sighed; she wanted to tell the kittens that

wasn't her problem. But like her captain, she had a duty to all of the passengers on the ship, and she supposed that included these kittens. Besides, the little one—Cosmo—didn't look as if he would last five minutes without a grown cat to keep him out of trouble.

"I'll take you somewhere safe," Clara said finally. "But you must stay out of trouble and out of sight. If you are discovered, I won't be able to help you. Do you understand?"

The three kittens nodded in unison and Jack gave Clara a wide grin, as though he'd known all along that she was going to help them.

Clara poked her head out from beneath the cover and scanned the deck. It was teatime, so most of the passengers were in one of the dining rooms. "The coast is clear," she told the kittens. "Follow me as quickly as you can. If I tell you to hide, you hide."

The kittens nodded again and jumped one by one up onto the wooden bench inside the lifeboat, their tiny claws gripping the sides as they tried to keep their balance. Cosmo didn't quite make it, and his paws slipped off the edge. Clara watched him scrabble helplessly inside the boat for a few moments, then tutted before gripping the scruff of his neck gently with her teeth and lifting him up next to his brother and sister. "This is why I never had kittens," she muttered to herself. "It's a bit of a drop for you on the other side," she told them. "So do try to land on your feet."

She needn't have worried. As she landed soundlessly on the deck, the three kittens followed swiftly behind, each of them landing with the same grace—even Cosmo, who looked particularly pleased with himself. Clara stopped herself from smiling, then took another survey of the deck.

"All clear," she whispered. "Quickly, now."

She ran along the freshly polished wood of the promenade, the kittens' tiny paws pattering behind as they kept close to the edges, ducking beneath the numerous deck chairs and benches, until they reached the captain's quarters. The captain always left his door slightly ajar so that Clara could come and go as she pleased.

His quarters were made up of three rooms: the bathroom (which Clara rarely ventured into), complete with a bathtub; the bedroom, with a bed and a large, carved wooden wardrobe where the captain kept his uniforms; and a sitting room with a table and chairs and a comfortable settee where Clara took most of her naps. In the late afternoon, the sun shone through the porthole, hitting the perfect spot.

Clara turned to the kittens, whose eyes were wide as they took in the luxurious surroundings. The walls were paneled with mahogany and intricate wallpaper, with crimson curtains made of silk, and the furniture was just as grand, made from the finest oak and upholstered in the richest of fabrics. Not to mention the plush cream carpet, which Clara loved to sink her paws into.

"These are the captain's quarters," Clara told them. "You'll have to stay here for now, until I find more suitable accommodations, but under no circumstances are you to leave this room, and when you hear the captain, hide silently beneath the table."

Violet looked at the large table, then back at Clara. "What will happen if he finds us, Miss Clara?"

Clara wasn't sure. She hoped that the captain would let them stay until they reached land, but she would feel much happier if they were somewhere they wouldn't be discovered by humans.

"The captain is a very busy man," she told them. "He rarely spends much time in here, apart from cleaning himself and sleeping, so you should be fine."

Cosmo nudged Clara's leg with his nose. "I'm hungry, Miss Clara," he mewed.

Jack and Violet nodded.

Clara sighed. "Stay here and out of sight. I'll see if I can scrounge something from the galley."

She turned to leave, already regretting having brought them to her captain's quarters, but unsure of anywhere else where they would be safe. She hurried down into the depths of the ship toward the galley, hoping that the kittens wouldn't rip the place apart while she was gone.

CHAPTER 6
MUTT

Thursday, April 11, 1912

"What do we have here?" a loud voice asked, startling Mutt awake.

"I think it's a stowaway," another voice said with a laugh.

Mutt jumped up, growling at the two men dressed in navy uniforms with small caps upon their heads, who peered down at him with puzzled expressions.

"Easy, boy," one said, reaching down to stroke Mutt's head.

Mutt felt himself relax a little, relief flooding through him as he realized that he wouldn't starve after all. But before he had the chance to gather his nerve to make a run for the open door, the other man had sneaked up behind him and looped a long length of parcel twine around his neck.

Mutt struggled against the tether. It cut into his neck. "Calm down, boy," the man said, stroking his head again. "We're not going to hurt you."

"What are we going to do with him, Billy?" the other man asked.

"He can keep us company," Billy replied, scratching Mutt behind the ears. "He reminds me of my old dog back home."

The other man snorted. "A mail dog?"

He lifted some sacks and hauled them over his shoulder, pausing as he reached for the one Mutt had been sleeping on.

"He's gone and done his business all over the mail!" he yelled.

Mutt's tail drooped between his legs and his head hung in shame. It wasn't his fault—there had been nowhere else to go.

Billy ignored him. "We can clean it up. It's only on the sack; no one will ever know."

The other man grunted. "Well, I want no part of it. If

you want to take on a stowaway, he's your responsibility—that means the mess he's made an' all."

Billy smiled at Mutt and led him out into the corridor. "He's just scared and hungry. I wonder how he came to be locked up in here?"

Mutt's tail wagged as he took in his new surroundings. He sniffed at the air, the floor, the walls, searching for any scent of Alice or the master. They continued up a flight of stairs, past a sign on the wall that read G DECK, then along a corridor to a door marked POST OFFICE. At one side of the wall were rows of sacks full of mail to be sorted; across the back wall and down the other side were rows and rows of shelves with small cubbyholes where hundreds of letters and small parcels had already been placed.

Billy laid a blanket on the floor for Mutt. Then he pulled from his pocket a small package wrapped in brown paper and held it out. Mutt sniffed at it cautiously—and then it hit him. The sweet scent of salted roast beef. He snuffled his jaws inside the package, gobbling up the sandwich without taking a breath.

"Easy, easy!" Billy laughed. "There's more where that came from." He nodded to the huge sacks behind him. "I've just got to sort through this lot first, then I'll see what else I can find you."

Mutt glanced at the door, which was still ajar. Billy must have caught his intention, though, because he swiftly closed it. "Best you stay with me for now," he told Mutt. "The captain won't be too pleased if he finds out I'm harboring a stowaway."

He patted Mutt on the head, then turned to his work. The way he moved from one task to another, sorting letters and parcels faster than Mutt's eyes could keep up, was quite soothing. The room was warm and the blanket beneath Mutt soft. With no immediate way to escape, Mutt found himself drifting off to sleep again.

Sunday, April 14, 1912

Mutt stayed in the post office for what felt like forever. Every so often Billy would feed him, occasionally letting him out for a quick walk along the corridor on his makeshift leash. He spread a pile of newspaper in the corner for Mutt to do his business—despite the other mail workers' protests—but he was always careful not to let Mutt near the door. And whenever he left Mutt alone, Billy would lock the door behind him.

As the days ebbed painfully away in an endless cycle of letter and mail sorting, so did Mutt's hopes of ever finding Alice again. Until, on the fourth day, Billy made a mistake. Mutt lay quietly on the blanket pretending to be asleep, waiting for his chance to escape.

"Can you help me with that big parcel in the mail-room?" a man called from the open door. Billy nodded, then glanced down at Mutt. Mutt let out a big snort of a snore, and Billy laughed, then followed the other man.

Mutt opened one eye, chancing a peep at the door. Just as he'd hoped, it was still open! He jumped up as quickly as he could, his claws slipping on the blanket as he darted to the doorway and out into the corridor.

Mutt sprinted along, all his senses on high alert. The passengers would most likely be up on the higher decks, so that was where he intended to begin his search. Ahead of him, a narrow stairway led straight up. Mutt waited for a moment, then charged up the stairs to the next level, labeled F DECK. Here, he could hear the thrum of the engines and the vibration beneath his feet as they powered ahead. He raced up the stairs to the deck above—E DECK.

The corridor ahead ran as far as Mutt could see. Mutt took a deep breath and wondered how on earth he was going to find Alice. It could take him a month to search a single deck, let alone the entire ship. The chatter of human voices drifted toward him and Mutt froze. After a couple of beats, the voices faded away in the opposite direction.

"Where have you been!" a voice yelled behind him.

Mutt spun, his hackles raised, but the corridor was empty. For a moment the only sound was his heart thumping in his ears, but then he heard a tutting sound followed by a small huff.

"Over here!"

Mutt sniffed along the wall to a small, louvered vent at the bottom. "King Leon?"

The rat's bright black eyes peered back.

"I've been searching for you all over the ship!" King Leon squeaked.

"I was trapped in the post office," Mutt said. "But I escaped, so I'm going to find Alice—my girl." Mutt started off in the opposite direction.

"You can't just go wandering around the ship in the middle of the day!" King Leon squealed.

"I have to find her," Mutt said. "I've lost enough time already."

"Sure, sure," King Leon said. "But what was the plan? Just go mingle with the humans until you find her? You need to be patient. Wait until the humans are asleep, then we'll have the run of the ship."

Mutt's head dropped. He knew King Leon was right, but he was so desperate to see Alice that it hurt. His belly ached as it grumbled loudly. Billy hadn't fed Mutt that morning, and he was starting to feel light-headed.

"Hungry?" King Leon asked.

Mutt's stomach gurgled again in response and he heard another loud sigh from the vent.

"Fine." King Leon huffed. "I tell you what, I am a little peckish myself, so if you don't mind taking a bit of a risk, we *might* be able to find something to eat now. But you have to do exactly what I tell you—first sign of any humans, and I'm off. You got it? It'll be every rat, or dog, for himself."

"Got it!" Mutt agreed, his tail wagging.

"Wait there," King Leon said.

There was a pitter-patter of tiny paws on metal as King Leon scuttled away from the vent. A few seconds later, he reappeared at an opening in the wall at the far end of the corridor and waved a paw at Mutt.

Mutt hurried down to find the rat waiting in the middle of an open room covered with an ornate metal-barred gate. It appeared to be a cage of some sort, and after being held in the post office for four days, there was no way he was going to walk straight into another prison.

"You coming?" King Leon whispered.

Mutt didn't move. "This room is empty," he said, confused. He'd thought they were heading for a food store.

King Leon sighed. "It's called an elevator. The humans use it to go up and down. Trust me—it will take us where we want to go."

Mutt frowned and backed away. It had to be some kind of trap like the ones the master used to snare rabbits.

"I think I'll take my chances on my own," he said, glancing around for a safer option.

"Like I said, it's a bit risky," King Leon said. "But

this way's a lot safer than traveling along Scotland Road. Too many humans about."

"Scotland Road?"

"It's what the humans call this long corridor. The crew use it to get to other parts of the ship." King Leon raised his head, his whiskers twitching. "The elevator operator's coming back. Get in!"

Mutt didn't wait to be told twice. He eased himself through a gap between the metal bars. It was a tight squeeze—especially for his head—but luckily his belly was empty and he landed on the floor of the elevator.

"Under here," King Leon called from beneath a bench covered in plush red fabric, set into the back of the elevator.

Mutt had barely tucked himself underneath the bench when a human appeared, pulling the metal gate open to step inside the cage.

"What now?" Mutt whispered.

"Hold on to your stomach," King Leon whispered back. "We're on the move."

CHAPTER 7
MUTT

Sunday, April 14, 1912

"Going up!" the man called out as a couple more humans stepped into the cage.

Mutt backed up as far as he could go. "You said this way would keep us away from the humans!" he growled through gritted teeth. "Now we're surrounded by them!"

"Not for long," King Leon replied. "Trust me."

The cage suddenly lurched. On the other side of the metal gate, the corridor floor seemed to sink as the cage rose, higher and higher, until the corridor disappeared altogether. There was only the dimmest of lights, which didn't seem to come from any oil lamp or flame that Mutt could see.

It felt to Mutt as though they were moving inside the very walls of the great ship. He sank his claws deep into the plush carpet. They were trapped. He would be forever trapped inside the walls of the *Titanic* with a rat.

Along the top of the cage, a sliver of bright light appeared. It grew brighter and brighter until they arrived at an open foyer. The cage finally came to a stop with a slight jolt, and the man who seemed to be controlling the box pulled open the metal gate, freeing the humans.

Mutt took a step forward, but King Leon placed a paw on his tail. "Wait...."

"I need to get out of here," Mutt breathed, desperate to escape.

The elevator operator stepped out and stood guard on the outside, seeming to be waiting for something.

"Try not to draw attention to yourself," King Leon whispered, racing out of the elevator without a second glance back at Mutt.

"Easy for you to say," Mutt mumbled. The humans were much more likely to spot him than they were a rat. He waited for a moment to make sure the man's back was still turned, then he ran with trembling legs as his stomach lurched from fear, or hunger, or both.

He turned the corner and paused at the top of the grandest staircase he had ever seen. It was carved from wood and inlaid with twisted metal and colorful glass. At the bottom was a curious statue of what looked like a small naked child holding a lamp. High above, a huge glass dome flooded the interior of the ship with light.

Mutt shook himself out of his reverie and turned, almost colliding with a woman wearing a large hat covered in colorful feathers, who shrieked in surprise. Mutt hurried on, wondering what sort of bird had had to die so that she could wear that ridiculous hat. Finally, he spotted King Leon's rump bouncing in the distance and followed the rat along another corridor until he stopped beneath a trolley covered with dirty plates and cutlery.

"I was almost caught!" Mutt growled, his heart racing.

"I told you there was a bit of risk," King Leon wheezed. "Come on," he said, running through a doorway onto a large, open deck.

The sudden scent of the big blue and the blast of fresh air in his face almost knocked Mutt over.

"Where's...the land?" he gasped, feeling dizzy at the sight of so much water. There was nothing but the vast ocean in every direction.

Mutt crawled beneath a wooden deck chair, his head spinning and his stomach heaving as he realized that whether Alice was on board or not, there was no way off the great ship now. "I'm not sure this is a good idea after all," he groaned.

King Leon scuttled beneath the chair beside him. "I thought you were starving."

Mutt was about to say he'd suddenly lost his appetite, when he caught a delicious scent that made his mouth water, despite the queasy feeling in his stomach.

King Leon grinned. "You smell that?"

Mutt nodded. "What is it?"

"You think it *smells* good, wait till you taste it." King Leon scurried to the next deck chair, then the next, pausing for a second to glance back at Mutt. The rat jerked his head forward, and Mutt followed, moving beneath the deck chairs for cover. They paused again as a pair of humans paraded past, but there was no scream this time. The humans seemed to be completely unaware that Mutt was there.

"How do you know your way around so well?" Mutt asked.

King Leon shrugged. "I've been on a lot of ships.

Besides, rats just know these things—it's like a sixth sense or something. If you ever find yourself in a bad situation, follow the rats." He glanced around, then gestured to Mutt to follow. "This way."

Mutt snorted. *Follow the rats?* He'd been doing exactly that, and so far it had gotten him into more trouble, not less. Although if King Leon was leading him to food, he supposed the risk would be worth it.

He followed King Leon beneath a wooden bench. They were so close that he could almost imagine what the food would taste like once he had it in his jaws. He was so focused on the food that he didn't notice he had attracted some unwanted attention.

"What are you doing under there?"

Mutt jumped, banging his head against the underside of the bench. He turned and snarled at a tiny, fluffy dog not much bigger than King Leon.

"None of your business!" Mutt growled.

The little dog took a step closer, not sensing the warning beneath Mutt's growl. This was clearly a dog who had never been in a fight in his entire life.

"Where's your owner?" the dog asked, cocking his head to one side.

"She's...somewhere on the ship. Now, get out of here," Mutt growled again, baring his teeth in the hope that the dog would get the message. Normally Mutt would have given the dog a quick nip on the leg or rump to show him who's boss, but he couldn't afford to attract any more attention, especially not from the humans.

The dog sniffed, then narrowed his eyes. "I don't believe we've met. Are you traveling in second class?"

Mutt glanced over at King Leon, who gestured wildly at him to ditch the tiny dog. "Yes," Mutt lied.

"Fifi! Fifi, what are you doing under there?" a lady called out in a shrill voice.

Mutt couldn't help giving a bark of a laugh. "*Fifi?* What kind of a name is that?"

But the tiny dog wasn't paying attention to his owner—he was looking at Mutt's dirty, matted fur and at the lack of collar around his neck, and his tiny eyes widened. "You're a stowaway!" he barked loudly.

To the humans this would have sounded like a high-pitched yapping, but to Mutt it was a warning.

"Help!" the tiny dog yapped. "There's a feral dog on board—it might have fleas!" He looked at Mutt again and snarled in disgust. "Or *rabies*!"

"Nah," King Leon said, appearing beside Fifi, standing on his hind legs to make himself taller. "Mutt here doesn't have rabies...but I might. You know, they said it was us rats who caused the Black Death."

He snapped his teeth at the little dog and Fifi yelped, running off to his owner with his tiny tail between his legs. King Leon chuckled and watched him go, then sent Mutt a wink before heading in the opposite direction. Mutt gave a small smile despite himself, thinking that maybe having a rat as a friend wasn't all bad.

CHAPTER 8
CLARA

Sunday, April 14, 1912

Clara was exhausted. Only four days with the kittens and they were already running her ragged, not to mention the constant back-and-forth between them and her duties as ship's cat. Yesterday, Jack had accidentally soiled the captain's slippers. Clara had ended up taking the blame, which she was not at all pleased about, and this morning Cosmo had somehow climbed up onto the side of the empty bathtub and fallen in. He had been stuck there until Clara had rescued him.

It wasn't all bad, though. At night when they snuggled up against her for warmth and all was calm, Clara felt a quiet contentment. And when Jack had gotten himself stuck beneath the captain's hat, Clara had laughed so hard that she'd surprised herself.

She wearily headed back to the captain's quarters after a long session of ratcatching in the lower decks. She'd hoped to bring one back for the kittens, but the rats on board were quick-witted and she'd not managed to catch a single one.

"Where are your brothers?" Clara asked Violet as the kitten peeped out from beneath the table.

"They, um..." Violet stared at the floor, scratching with her paw at a small thread that had come loose from the carpet.

A sense of dread filled Clara's stomach. "Violet? I need you to tell me where your brothers have gone."

Violet's eyes brimmed with tears. "I tried to stop them, Miss Clara."

"Which way did they go?" Clara asked.

Violet nodded at the door. "They were hungry."

Clara turned to leave, then had second thoughts. "You'd better come with me," she told Violet. "I clearly can't trust any of you to be alone."

Violet padded along behind, her head hung low, and Clara felt a pang of guilt for having been so harsh. Violet wasn't to blame for her brothers' disappearance. That was the trouble with kittens, Clara thought with a sigh, they were *always* hungry.

She quickly caught up with Cosmo along the B deck, where the first-class restaurant and popular Café Parisien were located.

"Where do you think you are going?" Clara snapped.

Cosmo sniffed at the air. "I smelled something delicious," he said as his tummy gave a little grumble.

"Where is your brother?" Clara asked, searching the deck frantically for Jack.

"He was here a second ago," Cosmo said.

Clara hurried along the deck with Cosmo and Violet chasing after her. Up ahead, a little girl with bright blue ribbons in her hair held Jack in her arms. She was singing to him and rocking him as though he were a human baby.

Jack leaned his head back and saw Clara. "Help, Miss Clara. I'm being cat-napped!"

Clara turned to Cosmo and Violet. "Wait here," she told them. She raced ahead of the little girl, then gave a loud meow before throwing herself on the ground at the girl's feet.

"Oh!" cried the little girl, kneeling down to see if Clara was all right.

Clara rolled onto her back, wriggling her belly in the air and purring to tempt the girl. For a brief moment, Clara thought her plan had failed, but then the girl released Jack to give Clara's tummy a rub. Clara purred loudly, pretending she was enjoying the ordeal, as Jack sneaked away to join his siblings. As soon as he was out of sight, Clara quickly jumped up, running in the opposite direction to lead the girl away.

Once Clara was sure the girl was well and truly turned around, she returned to the kittens.

"Well!" Clara cried. "That was almost as humiliating as the slipper incident."

"We're sorry," Jack sniffed.

"We only wanted something to eat," Cosmo added.

Clara opened her mouth to berate them some more, but something else had caught her attention. She sniffed at the air, then froze.

The kittens copied her.

"Ugh!" Violet cried. "What is that awful smell?"

"It smells like...like..." Jack made a choking sound, unable to name the horrid scent.

"Dog," Clara spat, sniffing again as her sharp claws extended. "And a particularly unpleasant one at that, judging by the smell of it."

She tilted her head, and again the kittens copied her, listening carefully to the distant sound of hurried paw-steps coming their way. By her reckoning, Clara counted eight paws. Four were ever so light. Barely more than a whisper, they traveled along quickly as though they were running to, or away from, something. The other four were heavier, clumsy, and they carried with them the distinct reek of a filthy dog. Clara had already met most of the first-class dogs, and they had all been coated with some kind of perfume, smelling more human than animal. This one was different. This one smelled like the dogs who prowled the docks at night, scavenging the alleyways in search of food or a fight, and who seemingly never bathed.

This one smelled like danger.

"Wait here," Clara told the kittens, a mixture of fear and adrenaline racing through her. "Stay out of sight and do not move one whisker until I return."

She stayed low as she moved, following the stench along the deck. It was so strong it was almost overpowering. She finally caught sight of the furiously wagging tail of a scruffy mongrel hiding beneath one of the deck chairs outside the café. It seemed to be waiting or watching for something...probably food, Clara thought. Dogs' heads seemed to be filled with the thought of their next meal and not much else. Much like kittens.

Clara stalked closer, preparing to pounce, her hunting instincts taking over. Dogs were supposed to be kept in kennels on the F deck under the watchful eye of the carpenter, but some first-class passengers insisted on keeping their coddled pets in their cabins with them while the steward turned a blind eye. Clara, on the other hand, would do no such thing.

Whomever it belonged to, Clara thought, she couldn't have unaccompanied dogs wandering the ship as they pleased. She leaned back on her hind legs, ready to strike, then gave a sly smile, baring her teeth as she prepared to teach the dog a lesson it wouldn't soon forget.

CHAPTER 9
MUTT

Sunday, April 14, 1912

"I can fight my own battles," Mutt grumbled, getting as far away from the yappy dog as possible.

"Sure you can," King Leon said with a wink. "But we don't have time to chat with the upper class."

Finally, they reached the source of the mouthwatering smell. It was wafting out from an open doorway along the deck. Wicker chairs and tables were set out, and tall climbing plants wove in and out of painted white trellises along the walls. A few humans sat at a table farther away, but the table closest was empty. On it lay a plate with a half-eaten sandwich packed full of fresh, juicy meat and begging for Mutt to take a bite.

Mutt crept closer. He was so hungry he didn't care anymore if anyone saw.

"Save some for me!" King Leon squeaked behind him.

Mutt raised his front paws onto a chair and leaned forward, his jaws almost touching the sandwich. He was about to grab it and run as fast as he could to safety so that he could enjoy his meal in peace when King Leon gave a sudden loud warning squeal and scampered away. Before Mutt could figure out what had King Leon spooked, he heard an almighty screech. Razor-sharp teeth clamped down on the end of his tail. It was all he could do to not howl and give himself away to the nearby humans. He whipped around as fast as he could, expecting to see the yappy dog returning for his revenge, but all he could see was a blur of fur and teeth and claws, hissing and spitting as it attacked. Mutt tried to fight back, snapping his teeth at the creature until it finally released its deathlike grip.

Mutt spun to face his attacker, baring his teeth. Now that his tail was free, he knew the odds were in his favor. He was bigger and stronger, but the creature had the backbone to attack a dog twice its size, and judging by the wicked look in its eyes, Mutt knew it would be a dirty fight. The creature copied his stance in a standoff as they circled each other. It was something that Mutt had never in a million years thought he might find on a ship as grand as the *Titanic*.

The worst, most despised of all dogs' enemies.

A cat.

CHAPTER 10

CLARA

Sunday, April 14, 1912

"What are you doing on my ship?" Clara snarled at the mongrel. She wouldn't make the mistake of biting him again—her tongue felt like it was coated with wiry strands of fur. They prickled at her throat and had the distinct aftertaste of salt and rotten fish and something even nastier that she couldn't bring herself to name.

The dog's coat was long and matted. It was the kind of color that wasn't really a color at all—more a mix of various shades of dirt. His rat associate had long since scarpered. It was only her surprise at seeing a dog and a rat apparently in cahoots that had allowed the rat time to escape. Clara wouldn't let him get away that easily, though; she'd never seen such a plump rat. Perhaps she would teach the kittens a few of her hunting tricks— once she'd dealt with the dog.

"Your ship?" the dog growled in reply. "What do you mean, *your* ship?"

"I am the captain's cat," Clara told him. "It is my responsibility to take care of *stowaways* like you and your rat friend."

The dog glanced around, but the rat had scuttled off into hiding somewhere.

"Coward," the dog muttered under his breath. "I'm not a stowaway," he told Clara. "I'm here with my owner. I have as much right to be on this ship as any other dog."

Clara narrowed her eyes. "Liar," she spat. "If you have an owner, where is he or she? Dogs are not allowed to parade along the decks unaccompanied, and they are most certainly not allowed to scavenge scraps from the first-class dining areas."

At the mention of food, the dog stared forlornly at the sandwich he had been trying to steal, still sitting abandoned on a fine china plate decorated with the White Star insignia. Then, to Clara's surprise, he sighed and backed down.

"Maybe I don't have an *actual* ticket, but my girl *is* somewhere on this ship," he told her. "She's going to the New World. I didn't want her to leave without me, so I sneaked on board. I'm not here to cause any trouble; I just want to find my girl—Alice."

His words came out in such a garbled rush that Clara could hardly understand what he was talking about. Of course, dogs weren't the most eloquent of speakers at the best of times. She considered him for a moment, trying to figure out if he was stalling for time, trying to catch her off guard before he made a run for it, or if he really was telling the truth. Before she could make a decision either way, she was interrupted by a tiny squeak beside her.

"Miss Clara?" the little kitten mewed. "I'm hungry." Cosmo's gaze slid to the same sandwich that the dog had been after, and he licked his lips.

"Cosmo!" Clara cried. "I told you to stay hidden." She leaned down to whisper in Cosmo's ear so that the dog wouldn't hear her. "Didn't your mother teach you that dogs mean danger?"

Cosmo peered around Clara's legs at the dog, then slowly shook his head. "Mother didn't really teach us much of anything."

He sniffled, then took a step toward the dog and looked him up and down. Clara instinctively took a step forward. The kitten might not belong to her, but she wasn't about to let him get mauled by a street dog. The mongrel was clearly starving, and dogs would eat anything. But the dog cocked his head and gave Cosmo a dopey smile, his tongue half lolling out of the side of his mouth.

"He doesn't *seem* that dangerous," Cosmo said, giggling. "Smelly, maybe, but not dangerous. *Are* you dangerous?"

The dog chuckled, then shook his head. "You're in luck," he joked. "I only eat kittens on Saturdays."

Clara hissed at the dog, then froze as a waiter wandered over. She quickly ushered Cosmo beneath the tablecloth, out of sight. The dog followed, squeezing himself in beside Clara. They sat in silence as the waiter cleared the table above. As soon as the coast was clear, Clara shoved her head against the dog's shoulder to get him to move a little.

"My name's Mutt," the dog told Cosmo, backing up a little. "I won't hurt you—I promise."

Cosmo laughed and ran out from behind Clara's legs.

"I'm Cosmo!" he said. "This is Miss Clara—she's going to take care of us."

"Us?" Mutt asked.

"Cosmo!" Clara said sharply.

Cosmo ran over to his siblings, who were poking their heads out from behind a tall potted plant in the corner of the café. Clara quickly followed, with the dog trailing along behind her as if they were in some kind of pack. Clara wondered how it had come to this—only four days ago it had just been her and her captain. Now she was watching every stowaway on the ship.

"I told you to stay with us!" Violet hissed at Cosmo. She looked up at Clara. "I did, Miss Clara, I promise."

"Get out of sight before any humans see you," Clara said, nudging the kittens back behind the ornate planter. "You too," she ordered the dog, who had paused behind her.

Luckily, most of the passengers had gathered in the first-class restaurant, rather than the café, where the captain was conducting his usual Sunday-morning service of prayer and hymns.

"We're sorry," Jack mewed, not looking at all sorry.

Clara sighed. "We'll discuss it later. I need to decide what to do with this dog."

"He doesn't look so bad," Jack said. "Maybe you could look after him, too, Miss Clara?"

Clara choked at the thought, and the dog chuckled again.

"These kittens trust me," he said. "Maybe you should, too?"

Clara had narrowed her eyes, wondering if she should alert the captain or find the nearest officer, when she had a better idea. "I'll make you a deal," she said slowly.

Mutt cocked his head to one side. "What kind of deal?"

"In all my years with the captain, I've never let any stowaway remain on my ship," she said, not adding that she had never in fact ever come across any stowaways before—apart from rats, and they didn't count because they were easily dealt with. But here was a chance to deal with them all in one swift move and enjoy the rest of the voyage with her captain in peace.

"Cosmo and his siblings, here, are also...unaccompanied," Clara continued. "If you promise to watch them and keep them out of sight and out of trouble for the rest of the journey, I will promise to allow you and your rat friend to live."

Mutt started to protest, but Clara ignored him. "That means no more wandering the decks. You must remain hidden until we dock, and then and only then will you be allowed to find your girl—if she is in fact on this ship at all."

"But she doesn't know I'm here," Mutt barked. "If I don't find her on the ship, it will be impossible to find her in the New World."

"Ah, so the truth comes out! It's that or be thrown overboard," Clara snapped, running out of patience, and the kittens gasped.

Clara bit her tongue as the kittens gave her an uneasy look, but it was too late to take it back.

"What about them?" Mutt asked.

"What do you mean?"

"What happens to the kittens when we reach the New World?"

The three kittens looked up at Clara, apparently wondering the same thing. They were ever so young to have been abandoned by their mother, but that wasn't

Clara's fault. She couldn't look after them, and she certainly couldn't guarantee that the captain would want more cats around.

Clara avoided Cosmo's gaze as she gave the dog a steely glare. "That's not my problem," she said, turning to stalk away, her tail and nose high in the air. "Now, all of you follow me, before I change my mind."

CHAPTER 11
MUTT

Sunday, April 14, 1912

Mutt followed the cat down into the depths of the great ship. He wasn't entirely sure that she wasn't leading him into a trap, but he didn't have much of a choice. They finally arrived back at the lowermost deck, passing the mail storage room where Mutt had started his journey, then moving on to a large cargo area piled high with huge leather trunks and crates. There was even a shiny black motorcar.

"It's a little dark," Clara was telling the kittens. "But there is plenty of room for you to run about and the door is never closed, so you won't be shut in." She caught Mutt's eye as he gave her a glare.

"What about food?" he asked. "And where do we go to...you know...do our business?"

Clara sniffed. "I had the impression that dogs did their *business* wherever they pleased."

There was a loud squawk in the corner, and Clara and Mutt hurried over to see what the kittens were up to.

"What are you doing over there?" Clara called as Cosmo and Jack pawed at something out of sight.

There was another squawk and a ruffling of feathers, and Mutt moved closer to see Cosmo swiping at a large cage filled with chickens.

"Get away! Get away!" the birds clucked.

"Chickens?" Mutt said. "Why are there chickens down here?"

"They are cargo," Clara explained, ignoring the evil eye one of the chickens was giving her through the bars of the cage. "You're lucky that's all there is down here. I've been on voyages where there were pigs on board and, let me tell you, the smell is extremely unpleasant." She sniffed at Mutt. "Although it might not have bothered *you* so much."

Mutt bit his tongue, resisting the urge to snap back at the cat. He had to be patient and respectful. Let the cat think he would obey her every command and bide his time until she had wandered off to bother some other poor creature. Once the kittens were asleep, he would continue his search for Alice and return to them once he had found her. There was no way he could wait until they arrived in the New World. The sooner he found Alice, the sooner he would feel safe again.

Violet joined her brothers to tease the chickens with a wide, toothy grin. The chickens kicked their feet, stirring up sand and sawdust that billowed in the air in dusty clouds.

Violet and Jack coughed, moving to a safer position away from the fussing chickens, who rattled their cage back and forth. The kittens continued to give the chickens longing looks, even though the chickens were twice their size. Mutt wouldn't have minded a mouthful of chicken himself, but he preferred the roasted variety. Besides, he didn't think Clara would allow them to eat the humans' precious cargo.

"They are not for eating," Clara scolded the kittens, reading their minds.

At this, the chickens became more agitated, squawking and pressing their puffed-up bodies against the walls of their cage until it shook. An open crate perched on top of the cage wobbled. Before Mutt could move a paw, it toppled over onto Cosmo.

"Cosmo!" Clara screeched. She hurried over, glancing up at Mutt, whose heart was hammering in his chest.

"Cosmo!" he barked. "Can you hear me?"

"It's dark in here," Cosmo called out weakly.

"We need to lift the crate," Mutt barked, snapping Clara out of her shock.

Clara nodded. "We'll get you out of there, Cosmo." She looked at Mutt. "How are we going to lift it off him?"

Mutt searched for something they could use to pry the crate off Cosmo. In the corner he found another open crate filled with tall wooden sticks. He grabbed one in his jaws and carried it back to Clara, who paced the floor, assuring Cosmo that everything would be fine.

Mutt pressed his rump against the side of the crate, pushing with all his strength to ease up the edge. Then he quickly slid one end of the stick underneath.

"Help me lift this," he panted as Violet and Jack watched nervously.

Clara gripped the opposite end of the stick in her

teeth and Mutt did the same, shaking his head briefly at the absurdity of standing side by side with a cat.

"I'll help!" Jack said, biting the stick with his tiny teeth, and Violet joined him.

They gave one more heave, and the crate rose off the ground just enough to allow Cosmo to squeeze himself out. His fur was coated in a sticky golden substance, and he tumbled across the floor, rolling into a pile of chicken feathers.

"Are you all right?" Clara asked, examining Cosmo for any injuries.

"I think so," Cosmo said with a sneeze, sending feathers flying up around him.

Jack laughed. "He looks like one of the chickens!"

Mutt sniffed at Cosmo's fur, then gave his head a small lick. "It tastes...sweet," he said. "Like honey."

"Thank goodness you weren't crushed!" Clara said, nudging Mutt away to lick all the goo from Cosmo.

When he was clean, Cosmo snuggled up against Clara, too afraid to go near the chickens again. Violet and Jack snuggled against Mutt, and he settled down beside Clara, listening to the kittens' tiny purrs as they fell asleep.

"What are we going to eat down here?" Mutt asked. "We can't stay down here for days without food or water.... We'll be starved by the time we reach the New World." He paused for a moment, wondering if that had been the cat's intention all along. But then he saw how she looked at the kittens—always watching to make sure they were close by, nudging the smallest one—Cosmo— if he fell behind. If Mutt hadn't known better, he would have thought she was their mother. She might be happy to let Mutt starve, but she wouldn't let any harm come to those three kittens.

"Wait until nightfall," Clara told him. "I will bring you some food then. I can't do it while the humans are awake—it's too risky."

"What about my girl—Alice?" he asked. "I need to find her."

"You risked a lot to find her," Clara said.

Mutt nodded. "I can't imagine a world without her."

Clara gave him a small smile. "It's the same with my captain," she said. "We've been together since I was a kitten. I couldn't imagine being parted from him for even a few days."

"So you understand how I feel," Mutt said, hope

building in his belly for the first time since he boarded the *Titanic*. "You know this ship well....Maybe if we searched together...?"

Clara sighed. "I'll do what I can," she said. "But I have my duties, and these three to take care of." She eased her body away from the sleeping Cosmo and he rolled over to join his siblings, snoring against Mutt's fur. "The captain worries if I am away for too long. Please stay with the kittens for now," she said.

Mutt nodded down at the kittens sleeping against him. "I couldn't leave them even if I wanted to," he joked.

"Thank you," Clara said, and Mutt nodded in response.

She gave the kittens one last backward glance, and then she was gone, leaving Mutt thinking that maybe cats weren't as bad as he'd always thought.

CHAPTER 12

MUTT

Sunday, April 14, 1912

"Finally!" Mutt said as the kittens awoke from their naps. "Now, I don't know about you three, but I'm starving. Let's see if we can find something to fill our bellies with, shall we?"

Jack gave a loud meow in agreement, but Violet didn't seem so sure. "Miss Clara said we were to stay here," she said.

"She did," Mutt said. "But she also told me to tell you to do as I say, and I say that it's dark and cold down here and I'm so hungry that I'm not sure those chickens will be clucking for much longer."

The chickens overheard this and squawked loudly.

"We *could* find something to eat and be back here before Miss Clara even noticed," Jack said slowly.

"What if we get lost?" Cosmo asked.

"Miss Clara will find us," Jack told his brother. "She always does."

"Of course she will," Mutt agreed. "After all, she *is* the captain's cat."

The kittens followed Mutt out of the cargo hold and along the hallway, where the vibrations from the huge engines rumbled beneath their paws. As they moved along, Mutt felt the air warm, and they paused to peek into the open doorway of the boiler room, which was completely filled by its three huge furnaces. The heat coming from inside was incredible. Mutt watched for a moment as men loaded coal into the furnaces from a large bunker with shovels, back and forth, back and forth. Around their necks the men wore neckerchiefs, and every so often they sucked on the ends.

"No food in there," Mutt told the kittens, sniffing the air.

They went up a stairwell to the next deck, following their noses until they came to a doorway labeled THIRD-CLASS GALLEY.

Mutt peered into the large open kitchen. There were a couple of humans dressed in white uniforms and hats washing dirty dishes at the sink. Bubbling away on the stove behind them was a large steel pot, filled with something that made Mutt's stomach gurgle so loudly he worried for a moment that the humans might have heard.

"What is that smell?" Jack whispered, taking in a deep breath and sighing.

Mutt grinned at the kittens. "Our supper," he told them.

"How are we going to get to it?" Violet wondered aloud, licking her chops. Her wide eyes darted between the humans and the pot of food.

Mutt didn't have an answer to that. He just knew that if he didn't eat something soon, he would probably collapse and never wake up.

"Stay back!" he hissed as the humans dried their hands and turned toward the doorway. He ushered the kittens beneath his legs and they backed up, pressing themselves against the wall.

The humans came out of the galley, but to Mutt's relief, they turned the other way, moaning to each other about how much their feet hurt. Mutt waited for a moment, and when they didn't return, he gave the kittens a nod. "All clear!" he said.

They trotted into the galley and Mutt jumped up onto the metal counter beside the stove. He leaned his nose over the pot for a long sniff. It was filled with thick gravy and meat and vegetables and smelled so good it made him dizzy. Mutt lowered his tongue into the pot for a tiny taste but jumped back with a small yelp. "It's too hot!" he said, flapping his tongue about in the air to cool it.

"Maybe there's something else we can eat?" Violet suggested, wandering over to a large set of shelves piled high with plates, cups, and saucers.

Mutt suddenly caught the scent of something else a lot less appealing and jumped down from the counter.

"Who are your new friends?" a voice asked from the doorway.

Mutt didn't need to turn to see who was there. He had smelled him coming a good few minutes before he actually arrived.

"Come back to cause me more trouble, have you?" Mutt asked King Leon.

King Leon raised a paw to his chest innocently.

"Who, me?" he said with a grin. "I'm the one who's been getting you out of trouble, if you haven't noticed."

"Much good you did me when the captain's cat showed up," Mutt muttered.

"What was I supposed to do?" King Leon asked. "A yappy dog is one thing, but a cat—" He gave a little shudder. "No sirree, cats and rats do not mix well. That's one thing every ship rat knows. If the cat finds you, you're a goner." He gestured to his stump of a tail. "Trust me, I know. I almost got caught myself a few nights ago. But I'm here now, aren't I? Rats never abandon their friends."

Mutt looked at King Leon for a moment, deciding whether or not to forgive him. He *had* helped Mutt find a way onto the ship and had gotten rid of the yappy dog and led Mutt to food—even though he hadn't had a chance to actually eat it. "I suppose so," he said finally with a smile.

King Leon grinned, then nodded to the kittens. "How did you end up with these three?"

"It's a long story," Mutt sighed.

"Is that a rat?" Jack asked, running his tongue over his tiny, sharp teeth. "Can we eat him?"

Mutt cocked his head as though he was considering

Jack's request, and winked at King Leon, who smirked. "King Leon is a friend," Mutt said. "Friends are not to be eaten."

"How about some oodle instead?" King Leon said, scurrying to the far side of the galley.

"What's oodle?" Mutt asked as he and the kittens followed.

"It's a kind of stew," King Leon said, jerking his head up to the counter, where another batch of the delicious stew was cooling in smaller bowls set out on the steel table. "Made out of the leftover cuts of meat. The crew eat it because it's not good enough for the passengers."

Mutt helped the kittens clamber up onto the counter, his mouth watering and his stomach twisting at the sight, then he quickly followed.

"Well, it's good enough for me," he said, dunking his jaws into the nearest bowl and gulping down the meat, carrots, and gravy, barely stopping to chew or breathe until the bowl was empty. Then he licked it until it was as sparkling clean as the ones on the shelf. Beside him, the kittens were doing the same thing—although the chunks of meat were too big for their small jaws, so they lapped up the gravy as though it were milk.

After a few minutes, Cosmo looked at Mutt with a

dopey grin, sighing in satisfaction over his protruding belly.

King Leon caught Mutt's eye. The rat had stood up on his back legs, his whiskers twitching as he sniffed at the air.

"What is it?" Mutt asked. "Humans?"

King Leon frowned. "Something is not—" He didn't have a chance to finish his thought, because at that moment the humans returned. They took one look at the dog, rat, and three kittens eating their food and ran at them, screaming and shouting.

"Run!" Mutt barked, ducking as one of the humans swung an empty frying pan at his head.

The kittens jumped down from the counter and scrambled off in different directions before reuniting to run around the legs of one of the humans. The man spun around and around, trying to catch one of the furry blurs, until he became so dizzy he fell over, crashing into a pile of crockery, which smashed to the floor.

"Follow me!" King Leon puffed, racing along the counter to leap over the bubbling pot of oodle, barely making it to the other side.

The other human turned to give chase but tripped

over the broken crockery and knocked over a crystal bowl full of trifle, the contents of which landed on Mutt's head. Mutt licked the cream out of his eyes and raced after King Leon and the kittens, zigging and zagging along corridors and down the stairs, not stopping until they were back at the cargo hold.

"I think we lost them," King Leon puffed. He glanced up at Mutt and started laughing.

The kittens were lapping up the drips of cream that dropped to the floor from Mutt's fur. Mutt sighed, then licked away the cream and pieces of fruit and sponge cake seeping down his forehead as best he could. It was only when King Leon came over for a taste that he decided he'd had enough.

"I'm running out of time to find my girl," Mutt said. "We were almost caught. If I get trapped somewhere again—or worse—I'll never find her."

"So what's the plan?" King Leon asked, munching on a large chunk of strawberry that had fallen off Mutt's head.

Mutt had started to recount the whole story about Clara helping him to find Alice, when he heard the patter of tiny feet heading along the floor out in the hallway.

Five rats almost the same size as King Leon raced past. They shouted out something to King Leon in a language Mutt couldn't understand, then, seeing that he wasn't going to join them, hurried on.

Mutt turned to King Leon. "What was that all about?" he asked, wondering if Clara had found them and was on the prowl.

King Leon frowned and glanced back and forth along the corridor, his tail stump twitching as though he didn't know whether to stay or go after them. "I'm not sure. They're not Brooklyn rats, so I couldn't understand what they were trying to say, but..." His whiskers twitched in the air. "Remember what I told you? About rats sensing danger?"

Mutt nodded, an uneasy feeling rising in his stomach. "But there isn't any danger, is there?" he asked.

"Wait here," King Leon said, heading in the opposite direction to the other rats, despite what he'd said. "I'm going to investigate."

CHAPTER 13

CLARA

Sunday, April 14, 1912
11:35 PM

Clara padded silently along the deserted promenade deck, thinking about what the dog, Mutt, had asked. What would she do with the kittens when they reached land? If she turned them over to the humans, they might be separated, or worse. Maybe she could keep an eye on them on the return trip to Southampton and then see if she could find their mother? Clara wasn't sure, though, whether they'd found their way onto the ship in England or at one of their stops in France or Ireland. They might even have come from the shipyard where the *Titanic* was built in Ireland—that could explain how they'd gotten into the lifeboats. Clara shook her head to herself. The chances of the kittens ever finding their mother again were slim at best. Besides, all kittens left their mother sooner or later and had to learn to fend for themselves. It had been that way for Clara, and look at her now—a captain's cat on the finest ship in the world!

But . . . she thought, the kittens still weren't old enough or strong enough to fare well on their own on the streets, especially without a grown cat to teach them how to scavenge and hunt . . . and fight if they had to. Perhaps she might be able to somehow convince the captain to bring the kittens home with him? Maybe if she showed that she could be a kind of surrogate mother—or kitten-sitter, that would be better—and that they would be no trouble. There would be no more long trips on the ocean to consider, so that wouldn't pose a problem, and the captain had more than enough space to accommodate them all. Clara decided to think on it some more over the coming days. Maybe before they docked, she would introduce the kittens to the captain. She could even go so far as to try to convince him that they were her own. Surely he wouldn't abandon them then?

Clara continued toward the bow, slinking past the

few remaining first-class passengers—all men—playing cards and drinking in the smoking room. Most passengers had already retired for the night, as had the captain after a lengthy dinner held in his honor. The temperature had drastically dropped in the last couple of hours. Ice had begun forming on the windows, and many of the passengers who had been sunning themselves on the deck only that afternoon were now huddled inside their cabins to keep warm. The cold didn't bother Clara much. She'd been on enough voyages and had seen her way through enough storms to be hardier than most of the crew, let alone the fragile humans—especially the first-class passengers and their dogs, with their weak constitutions.

But then, Clara was unlike most cats, too. Most cats she had met wouldn't dare go near the water, let alone willingly sail across the ocean numerous times a month. Few would be suitable to be a ship's cat. Clara, however, felt as if she'd been born to live on the water. She couldn't imagine a life away from the ocean—the gentle, almost hypnotic sound of the waves lapping against the hull; the sweet tang of salt on the air; the gulls who called out to her when they were close to shore, welcoming her home.

Clara was looking forward to spending her final days with her master on solid ground, but she would miss moments like these, when she was free to wander the decks as though the vast ship belonged only to her and she was queen of the waves.

Clara looked up at the night sky. It was close to midnight—the time some humans called the witching hour, and the time when, on many voyages, Clara had seen the spectacle of colored lights playing in the sky like silk ribbons dancing on the wind, tempting her to chase them.

Tonight, though, there were no such lights. No moon, either. The sky was the clearest Clara had ever seen it, dotted with what seemed like a million twinkling stars. The sea, too, was just as clear and still. So clear that it was difficult to make out where the sky ended and the ocean began. There was no crest of a wave, no swell or imperfection ruffling its surface. It stretched out in front of the ship for miles as though they were sailing across an endless piece of polished glass at the very ends of the earth.

Clara decided that it was quiet enough for her to return to the kittens and bring them to the galley, where they might scrounge some scraps. The galley staff some-times worked late into the night, but one of the chefs had taken a liking to Clara, and she knew he would turn a blind eye to her if she needed him to. As she moved toward the stairwell, something rising above the water's surface in the distance caught her eye. The smallest glimpse of something out of the ordinary—like an imperfection in her vision. Something that moved and grew, slowly taking shape before her as it rose from the very depths of the ocean floor like a monster made entirely from ice.

An iceberg.

But this one was unlike anything Clara had seen before—usually, icebergs were easy to spot, reflecting the moonlight like beacons upon the water, but tonight there was no moon and so the iceberg appeared as black as the night itself. It was only her heightened ability to see in the dark that had enabled her to pick it out to begin with.

It loomed directly in the *Titanic*'s path as the ship sailed onward. Clara's fur prickled with fear. They were sailing too fast. They had to turn! Where was the warning bell from the lookouts? Why were the officers on the bridge not taking action and changing course?

Closer and closer, they sailed toward the iceberg. Toward danger.

Clara realized that she might be the ship's only hope. She shook away her fear and paused for a fraction of a second, unsure whether she should go directly to the bridge to alert the officers or to the crow's nest. If the captain was on duty, she knew he would take notice, but his officers dismissed her as nothing more than a glorified ratcatcher and would likely just shoo her away. She was already closer to the crow's nest than the bridge, so she decided to head to the lookouts.

She raced to the bottom of the crow's nest, which stood fifteen feet high, extending in a semicircle toward the bow of the ship. Clara leaned her head back to try to catch a glimpse of the lookouts; then she glanced out into the ocean. Any longer and it would be too late—if they continued dead ahead, they would almost certainly hit the iceberg directly.

Clara entered the hollow mast that led to the lookouts. Her claws scrabbled to climb the metal ladder set inside. Ordinarily, she was an excellent climber, but in her fear and haste, her claws slipped halfway up and she dropped to the ground with a screech, twisting and contorting her body into a landing position a second too late. She landed with a thud on her back leg. She heard the crack before she felt it. She tried to ignore the pain, turning immediately back to the ladder and attempting to climb again, but her throbbing leg gave way beneath her. The lookouts had still not spotted the iceberg. The brass bell above remained silent, and Clara had no way to warn anyone of the impending danger. No way to stop the catastrophe that was about to occur.

She took a deep breath and screamed a terrible high-pitched scream—one that she usually reserved for a fight over territory, or a piece of fresh fish—not out of pain or frustration, but to get the attention of the lookouts above. Surely they must have spotted the ice monster by now? Surely they would sound the alarm. Just as she had filled her lungs, ready to scream again and again until they took notice, the brass bell above rang out three times, sending a loud, vibrating echo around the foremast and through Clara's skull.

And to her relief, finally, she heard one of the men cry out: "Iceberg! Dead ahead!"

Clara sank to the floor, her throat raw and her body exhausted. She hoped they were not too late.

CHAPTER 14
CLARA

Sunday, April 14, 1912
11:40 PM

Clara allowed herself a moment to catch her breath before pulling herself to standing with a wince. Her leg pulsed with a painful heat that radiated up to her hip. She didn't think it was broken, though she had definitely done some damage. But she had no time to feel sorry for herself or to inspect her injury further. She had to wake the captain and alert him to the danger ahead. She half-hobbled, half-limped along the deck, trying not to set her injured back leg on the ground or place too much pressure on it.

The captain's quarters were directly behind the

bridge and wheelhouse on the starboard side, but by the time Clara had reached them, the captain had already been awoken and the quartermaster steering the ship was turning the wheel hard to starboard, away from the iceberg.

Clara held her breath as the nose of the great ship began to glide away, painfully slowly, from the iceberg that they were rapidly gaining on.

"It's going to be close," one of the officers said.

The captain made no reply. He left the bridge to stand outside for a clearer view. Clara followed him out onto the deck as they stared up at the huge iceberg bearing down upon them. "Hold on, Clara," the captain said, bending to lift her into his arms. He stroked her head gently, which seemed to calm them both.

For a moment it seemed as if they were going to be fine. It would be a near miss, but a miss nevertheless. But one thing Clara knew about icebergs was that often the tip—the visible part that rose above the water—was far smaller than the mass of ice that lurked below, and although there was no head-on collision, as Clara had feared, they did not miss it entirely.

There was a high-pitched screech that made Clara's

fur stand on end as the ship scraped past the very edge of the iceberg. The captain lost his balance and stumbled slightly, but he held Clara tightly, drawing her closer into his chest. His heart thumped as fast as Clara's as huge chunks of ice rained down upon the deck. The great ship swept past and the captain leaped out of the way, enclosing Clara within his arms to keep her safe from the shards of ice that scattered across the promenade.

Then, as quickly as it had seemed to sneak up on them, the iceberg was gone. When Clara looked back, all she could see was the darkness of the ocean and the starry sky above, as though nothing had happened. The captain lowered Clara to the deck, then strode back toward the bridge with Clara limping along behind.

Clara meowed, unable to keep up with him. The captain glanced back with a frown. "You're hurt!" he said, scooping her up again and examining her leg. "What have you been up to?"

There was a shout from the bridge and the captain hurried on, careful not to jolt Clara's leg.

"Stop the engines!" he called, and an officer sent the order down to the engine rooms. "We need to assess the damage."

The captain set Clara down by his feet. "Stay here," he told her. "I will tend to your leg once this is all dealt with."

The ship continued for a little way as the pistons driving the steam engines slowed to a stop. For a few breaths, all was eerily still and silent. The captain headed to the hull to find out what repairs needed to be made. Passengers awoken by the collision came out on the decks to see what was happening.

Despite what the captain had said, Clara couldn't wait to find out what had happened. She hobbled after the captain, watching some of the third-class passengers on the steerage deck, where most of the shaved ice had landed. A few of them laughed and played with the ice, throwing snowballs as if it were the first day of winter and nothing was amiss.

A barefoot girl in a thin nightgown caught Clara's attention. She had the brightest red hair Clara had ever seen. It bloomed among the dark and gray clothes of the other steerage passengers. The girl ran across to a large chunk of ice, struggling to break a piece off to show to a man who had come onto the deck with her.

"Look, Papa!" the girl called. "It's snowing! Can you believe it? In the middle of the ocean."

But the look on the girl's father's face told Clara that he knew as well as she that any kind of snow or ice on the deck of a ship was not a good thing. As Clara hurried on after the captain as best she could, she heard the father call the girl away.

"Come inside, Alice."

Clara froze. *Alice? Could this be Mutt's girl?* she wondered.

But there was no time to investigate. She finally caught up with the captain, who had been stopped by the same group of first-class passengers she'd passed in the smoking room. She hid beneath a chair so that he wouldn't reprimand her for following. He was reassuring them that all was well and they would be continuing on shortly, but to put on their life jackets. He told them it was standard procedure to halt the engines to check for any damage, and Clara heard one of the men proclaim: "How could there be any damage? We're on the unsinkable ship!"

The other men laughed in agreement, but the captain didn't share their humor, and when the chairman of the White Star Line, J. Bruce Ismay, joined them, Clara could see that he felt the same unease.

"We've hit an iceberg," the captain told Ismay. "We need to prepare the lifeboats. What is the damage, Thomas?" the captain asked the ship's architect as they headed back toward the bridge, with Clara trying her best to keep up.

"It's worse than I thought," Thomas replied. "The iceberg sliced a gash in the side of the hull that runs across at least four compartments—if not more. They're pumping the water out as quickly as they can, but it's coming in fast. I fear that some of the crew closest to the collision might already be lost."

"Close the watertight doors," the captain ordered the officer at the bridge.

"Already done, sir," the officer replied.

"I thought she was unsinkable?" one of the younger officers said.

The architect shook his head. "Only if the damage is restricted to one compartment. Any more than two or three, and the water will continue to pour in and eventually rise up and over, spilling into the next compartment, and so on. The doors are watertight, but the floor of the deck above is not. We need to start loading the lifeboats immediately."

The captain took the architect's elbow and gently pulled him to the side, out of earshot of the other officers. Clara followed, fearing the worst.

"How long have we got, Thomas?" the captain asked, his face as white as the ice on the deck.

The ship's architect caught Clara's eye. His own eyes widened in surprise at seeing a cat sitting there eavesdropping on the conversation. "With the amount of damage sustained by the hull plates, my estimate is that she's got two hours, maybe less, before the entire hull is flooded."

Captain Smith took a deep breath, then cleared his throat before turning back to his officers. "Send out a distress call to any boats in the area immediately. Tell them to come at once. The *Titanic* is sinking."

Clara didn't wait to hear any more. Water could be coming in that very second, and the kittens and Mutt might be trapped. She raced as fast as she could down into the ship, ignoring the fire in her leg and the fear building in her stomach, praying that when she'd taken the kittens into the hold, she hadn't led them to their death.

CHAPTER 15
MUTT

Sunday, April 14, 1912
11:40 PM

"What's happening, Mutt?" Jack called sleepily, his eyes still half closed.

"Is Miss Clara back?" Violet asked with a yawn, having been woken by her brother.

"Not yet," Mutt answered as he paced the floor, looking out along the corridor for any sign of King Leon. He didn't know much about rats or their sense of danger, but he could feel something himself. Something that he couldn't quite explain, deep in the pit of his stomach. He thought maybe it was just that he was tired or that his belly still wasn't quite full despite the three bowls of oodle he had demolished. Or maybe it was just that he hadn't found Alice yet, but the look in King Leon's eyes when he'd left made Mutt believe that it wasn't hunger causing his unease.

"Wake up, Cosmo," Mutt said. "We need to find King Leon or Miss Clara and see what's going on."

Violet nudged Cosmo with her nose, and he woke with a start.

"Follow me," Mutt told the kittens. "And stay close. If we see any humans, I'll distract them while you three head to the upper decks and find Miss Clara."

"I'm scared," Cosmo wailed.

"It will be fine," Violet told him. "Mutt will look after us, won't you, Mutt?"

Mutt wanted to say yes, but his throat felt too tight. Instead he gave Cosmo a quick nod, then trotted along the corridor to a spiral stairway, hoping it would lead to King Leon.

On the next level down, Mutt found himself back at the long corridor that King Leon had called Scotland Road. He gave a short, sharp bark, hoping that King Leon would hear, and waited for a few breaths. When the rat didn't appear, Mutt jerked his nose at the kittens and went down the next set of stairs onto F deck, past a room with a large pool, heading back toward the engines.

His ears pricked up as he heard something—a creaking noise that rose above the rumble of the engines and the firemen in the boiler rooms still loading the coal into the furnaces. It was almost like the scraping of claws down metal, but louder. Much, much louder. The ground beneath their feet shook and the great ship rattled and shuddered as though it had run aground.

"What is that?" Violet squeaked, huddling close to her brothers.

Mutt opened his mouth to answer, then he spotted King Leon racing toward them at full speed.

"What is it?" Mutt asked, his hackles raised. "What was that noise?"

King Leon held up a paw as he tried to catch his breath, but he didn't need to say anything, because at that moment, a river of rats ran past them. Mutt counted thirty at least. They were closely followed by the distinct sound of rushing water, like the tide upon a pebble beach, which made his fur stand on end.

"We. Need. To. Run," King Leon panted.

Above their heads a light flashed red. Wailing alarm

bells rang out, echoing around the corridor and deafening Mutt so that he could barely hear the kittens' screams. Mutt ran to them and crouched down. "Jack, Violet, climb onto my back and hold on. Any way you can— even if you have to use your claws," he barked quickly.

Then he grabbed Cosmo by the scruff of his neck, hoping he wouldn't hurt the kitten. Mutt bolted as fast as he could with two passengers clinging to his back, trying not to choke on Cosmo's fur, which tickled his tongue and throat. King Leon scurried after them, then to Mutt's surprise overtook them to take the lead. "Follow me!" he shouted back as the alarms continued to wail around them.

Ahead, Mutt could see that the doorway seemed to be lowering toward the ground. He paused for a second, putting Cosmo carefully down. "What's that?" he asked. "What's happening?"

"They're closing the watertight doors!" King Leon said. "This is bad. This is very bad. We have to get through before the water reaches us."

Mutt glanced behind them. "Too late!" he said, scooping Cosmo up again in his mouth as water seeped along the floor, creeping toward them.

He overtook King Leon and sprinted toward the door as it lowered to the ground. The space between the bottom of the door and the floor was getting smaller and smaller each second. For a moment, Mutt didn't think they would make it. He felt a flash of fear that they would be crushed by the thick metal door. He dived forward, hoping the kittens would keep their grip, sliding between the smallest of gaps and sending Violet and Jack flying over his head to tumble onto the floor in front of him in a furry heap.

"Is everyone all right?" he asked after he set Cosmo down. "Violet? Jack?"

Cosmo nodded, but he was shaking all over. Violet stood up and sent Mutt a glare that said she didn't appreciate being thrown around, and Jack gave him a small nod.

"Where's King Leon?" Cosmo asked in a small voice, barely more than a squeak.

Mutt spun around to look down the corridor, but it was no longer there. In its place was a steel door meters thick, cutting them off from the stairwell that led to the upper decks. And King Leon.

CHAPTER 16
MUTT

Monday, April 15, 1912
12:25 AM

"King Leon!" Mutt barked. "King Leon!"

He sniffed around the edges of the steel door and along the walls, hoping to find a vent or pipe that King Leon might have crawled through.

"Maybe he turned back and found another way out?" Mutt said to the kittens. But his hope faded as he heard King Leon's voice call out to him.

"Mutt!" King Leon shouted, his voice muffled by the thick door. "The water's coming in fast. Take the kittens as high as you can. Remember what I told you—follow the rats."

"What about you?" Mutt asked.

There was a pause, and for a moment Mutt was afraid that King Leon had been washed away by the water, but then his voice came back more clearly. It sounded slightly echoey but closer.

"I think I've found a way out," King Leon puffed. "But Mutt...if I don't make it out...If I can't..." There was a long pause, and Mutt feared the worst, but then King Leon's voice rang out again. "Remember I said I might ask you for a favor one day? In return for me helping you onto the ship?"

Mutt nodded, even though he knew King Leon couldn't see. "I remember," he answered. Although much good it had done him—he hadn't found Alice, and now it looked as though he was going to end up drowned anyway.

"I want to call in that favor now," King Leon said. "Just in case."

"King Leon, we can talk about this later. We need to get above decks and away from the water."

"Wait!" King Leon shouted. "Please..."

"I'm still here," Mutt said.

"Mutt," King Leon started. "Did you know that rats

don't live very long? A few years at the most. I'm an old rat, Mutt. I've been back and forth on these ships more times than I can count, and I've seen so many different places and met so many different friends along the way—like you," he added.

Mutt gave a small smile.

"I've lived a good life, Mutt," King Leon said. "And I want the same for you and those kittens—and your girl, Alice. Will you promise me that?"

Mutt's stomach dropped. "That's the favor?"

"I guess so," King Leon said with a small chuckle. "And if you ever find yourself in Brooklyn, tell my family I was a hero."

Mutt's chest felt tight but he answered anyway. "I will," he said, wishing with all his heart that King Leon were on this side of the door with them. "King Leon?"

"Yeah, buddy?"

"Thank you for helping me," Mutt said. "I'm sorry I called you a stinking rat. You are a hero to me."

He waited for a moment, but King Leon didn't reply.

"Mutt!" Violet screamed from behind him. "Look!"

Water had started streaming out through the slatted vents and pouring down the walls. In seconds it had risen over their paws, until it seemed to swallow up the carpet entirely.

"Let's go!" Mutt said. "King Leon, if you can still hear me, I hope you make it out."

He turned and crouched low so that Violet and Jack could climb onto his back again, and grabbed Cosmo's scruff in his mouth. Then he splashed through the frigid water, turning left and right, and left again, trying to remember where the stairwell was. When he reached the end of the corridor, his heart dropped as he found himself at a dead end where another steel door had cut off the hallway.

"We're trapped!" Jack shouted.

Mutt searched around, desperately trying to find higher ground. He cocked his head and listened for a moment. Then he heard a small squeak. *Rats!* he thought. *Follow the rats.* He turned and splashed back the way they had come, this time turning left. The water was up to his knees now. Ahead he saw a service trolley sitting outside another closed door.

Mutt stopped alongside and gestured with his head to the trolley, waiting for Jack and Violet to climb on. Then he let go of Cosmo, gently placing him beside his siblings. "Wait here," he told them. "I'm going to find a way up, and then I'll come back for you. It will be quicker if I go alone."

"Don't go!" Violet squealed, her whole body shaking.

"I won't be long, Violet, I promise," Mutt panted. "Jack will take care of you while I'm gone."

Jack gave Mutt a solemn nod, despite the fact that his jaw was trembling and his eyes were wide with fear. "I'll look after them."

Mutt splashed back down the corridor, trying to recall which way they'd come when Clara had led them down. There were no signs of any rats now—they had probably already reached the upper decks, Mutt thought. Or...he didn't let himself think of what else might have happened to them, because then he'd have to think about King Leon. Mutt *had* to believe that King Leon would find a way out. That he would see him again with that silly toothy grin of his and that stump of a tail.

But at the next corridor he found only more closed doors and more dead ends where the hallways were cut off by the watertight barriers, which, it turned out, were not so watertight after all.

A loud squeal echoed down the hallway far behind

him, and Mutt turned to race back to the kittens. It was almost impossible to move fast now. His legs and fur were weighed down by the rising water and his feet barely touched the floor. It felt as if he were wading through thick snow.

"Mutt!" Cosmo cried as he saw Mutt heading toward them. "It's Clara!"

Mutt sighed with relief and spun around, looking for the captain's cat. She would be able to lead them to safety. "Where?" he asked.

Cosmo sniffed at the air. "I...I don't know." He frowned. "I can smell her, I'm sure I can. She smells just like Mother."

Mutt glanced at Violet, and she gave a slight shake of her head.

Mutt's tail drooped, the tip dunking beneath the cold water, making his breath catch in his throat. "I'm sure she will come," he told Cosmo quietly. "We'll wait here for her."

There was nothing else he could say. Nothing else they could do. There seemed to be no way up or out. He couldn't carry the three kittens through water this high, and he certainly couldn't swim. They would weigh him down, and they would all drown before he got much farther than the next hallway.

Cosmo saw the defeated look in Mutt's eyes and stood up on the trolley so that they were eye to eye. "She will come," he said sternly, his voice steady and sure. "Miss Clara would never abandon us."

"Mother did," Violet said solemnly.

"Miss Clara is different," Jack told his sister. "She is the captain's cat. She would never leave a shipmate behind."

Mutt started to say that she was probably caught up with the captain when Cosmo stood up to yell at the top of his lungs, almost deafening Mutt. "Miss Clara! Miss Clara! We are here!"

Mutt shook his head as Jack joined in. After a pause, Violet began yelling, too. Mutt barked as loudly as he could, adding to the racket they were making in the hope that someone—*anyone*—might hear them.

CHAPTER 17
CLARA

Monday, April 15, 1912
Midnight

Clara raced down to the cargo hold as fast as she could with her injured leg, to where she had left Mutt and the kittens, but when she reached the corridor, the water-tight doors were already down, blocking her from going into the next compartment. There were no humans around, and already water had started to seep along the floor. She hobbled back up to E deck and along Scotland Road to the emergency stairwell to head back down to the cargo holds, hoping that the dog had had enough sense to move the kittens as soon as the ship had struck the iceberg.

When she descended, she found herself in the same predicament. This corridor, however, seemed to be filling up much faster than the previous section. Clara peered up at the metal barrier separating compartments and hoped nobody was trapped behind it. She had turned to climb back up the stairs when she heard a small cry coming from down the hallway. She paused, looking at the water. It was already a few feet high, certainly too high for her to wade through, not that she wanted to. Although she had been forced to swim once before (when she was a young cat and had accidentally lost her footing walking up the gangplank onto a smaller ship, and had ended up having to swim to the jetty to save herself), it wasn't an experience she particularly wanted to repeat.

She had almost convinced herself that she had simply imagined it, when she heard her name being called: "Miss Clara! Miss Clara!" Accompanied by the earsplitting noise of a barking dog.

Clara's heart froze. It was Mutt, and Cosmo. If they were somehow trapped along the corridor, they would have no way of escaping. She had to help them! She took a deep breath and jumped into the freezing water, her paws barely scraping against the waterlogged floor as she paddled back and forth frantically. Clara couldn't bear the thought of anything happening to the kittens. She just hoped she could reach them in time.

She turned one corner, then another, her claws scrabbling along as she tried to propel herself faster. *Where are they?* Finally, around the next corner she found Mutt trying to keep his head above water beside a service trolley on which the kittens were precariously balanced. They were shaking from fear and cold as the water rose rapidly around them.

Mutt noticed Clara and barked again, his eyes wide with surprise, then he turned to the kittens, whispering calming words to each of them.

"We couldn't find a way out!" he told her. "The ship is a maze."

Clara lifted her head, trying to keep her mouth and nose out of the water. The freezing temperatures had at least numbed her injured leg slightly, and she found that it was actually easier to move in the water than out of it.

"There's a narrow stairwell this way," she managed to spit out between breaths. "The water is rising fast, though, so we have to hurry."

She rested a paw on the bottom shelf of the trolley,

which was submerged, and managed to pull herself out of the water to crouch, shivering, beside the kittens. "Cosmo, can you climb onto my back?" she asked.

Cosmo looked up at Mutt, then peered down at the water and shook his head.

Mutt nudged Cosmo gently with his nose. "We'll be right behind you," he said gently.

Clara gave Mutt a grateful smile, then gestured to Violet and Jack. "Can you take these two? I don't think I can manage them all without being sunk myself."

Mutt nodded, and Violet and Jack carefully clambered once again onto his back. Clara saw him wince as they dug their tiny, razor-sharp claws into his skin, but he didn't utter a word of complaint.

"Stay close," Clara said, easing herself gently back into the water after Cosmo had settled onto her back.

The water had already risen by another few inches, and Clara struggled to keep both herself and Cosmo above the water so that they could still breathe. After a number of twists and turns, they reached the stairwell, and Clara finally felt solid ground underneath her paws. She thought she might collapse then and there in blessed relief.

Cosmo jumped from her back and scrambled onto the first available dry step, with his brother and sister not far behind. To her surprise, Mutt waited for Clara to pull herself out of the water before he followed. Being a fair bit bigger than her, he was able to keep his head out of the water when his paws touched the bottom stair—although if they stayed there for much longer the water would rise over his head.

Clara shook herself as dry as she could manage, then turned to Cosmo. "How did you know I was down here?" she asked.

"Your scent," he replied, his teeth chattering together with the cold. "You smelled a bit like how I remember Mother smelling."

Clara blinked at Cosmo for a moment, wanting to correct him to make sure there was no confusion. To tell him that she was not now, nor could she ever be, a replacement for his mother, but the water was still rising fast and the time for worrying about their future was long gone. She needed to make sure that the kittens survived the night. That was all that mattered.

"What happened?" Mutt asked, pulling Clara from her thoughts. "Why is there water pouring into the ship?"

"We hit an iceberg," she replied, turning her back on the kittens briefly so that they wouldn't hear. "Mutt, the ship is sinking fast. The humans are already loading the lifeboats on the top deck. We have to make sure the kittens get on one with them, but I'm afraid we don't have much time."

"What about my girl?" Mutt asked. "I need to find her and make sure she gets onto a lifeboat, too."

"If you help me with the kittens, I'll help you find your girl," Clara said.

Mutt glanced back at the kittens and nodded. "Let's go."

Clara led them back up to the boat deck, where the officers and crew had already begun to load the first lifeboats with humans. One of the officers was shouting out: "Women and children first!"

Some humans waited patiently in line to get into the lifeboats, first-class passengers mainly. But for some reason that Clara couldn't fathom, many others seemed reluctant to get into the lifeboats despite the peril they were facing, choosing to take their chances on the doomed ship. Clara turned away from the bow, toward the boats farthest away, which the officers hadn't yet begun to load. The covers had already been removed in preparation for launching, and Clara nudged the kittens toward the closest boat. It was the same lifeboat that she had found them hiding in, and she could still smell the faint scents they had left behind, lingering like a distant memory, even though it had only been four days ago.

"Do you remember where I found you?" Clara asked the kittens.

Violet watched the ever-increasing commotion at the front of the ship with wide eyes, while Jack and Cosmo nodded slowly.

"I need you to be brave, Violet," Clara said to get her attention. "Can you do that for me?"

"I'm scared," Violet said.

"There is nothing to be scared of," Clara told her. "You three are exactly like me—sea cats. And if I am the captain's cat, that makes you three my officers and second-in-command. I need you to stay inside this lifeboat to make sure that the passengers stay in line." She glanced over at Mutt. "And if any dogs happen to join you on board, you make sure to keep an especially close eye on them. You know how disobedient those dogs can be."

"I'll keep you safe," Jack told his brother and sister, and Clara felt a small burst of pride in the small but fearless kitten.

Mutt's eyes shone back at her, and he gave a small bark to clear his throat. "We need to hurry," he said. "The humans are moving closer."

"Come along," Clara said, nudging the kittens closer to the boat. "I will lift you into the boat. Now, this is important: I want you to make sure you remain hidden beneath the wooden bench. There should be some blankets that you can hide under to keep you warm."

She grabbed Jack by the scruff of the neck first and lifted him over the rim of the boat, then Violet. She reached down for Cosmo, but he backed away. "What about you, Miss Clara? And Mutt? Will you stay with us?"

"Cosmo," Clara said, gently rubbing her head against his. "I am the captain's cat. I still have work to do here on the ship, making sure all the other animals get safely away."

"But we'll see you again, won't we, Miss Clara?" Violet squeaked, jumping up onto the bench and peering up at her with those beautiful blue eyes.

Clara felt her heart break into tiny pieces. She didn't want to lie to the kittens, but she couldn't tell them the truth, either. Before she could find the words to tell them that this was goodbye, Mutt interrupted.

"Miss Clara will do her best to find her way back to you," he said. "So will I."

Clara nodded back at the dog gratefully, feeling sorry that she had ever judged him so harshly. Then she leaped up beside the lifeboat, and Mutt helped lift the kittens toward her. Clara carefully took the scruff of Cosmo's neck in her jaws and placed him in the boat beside his siblings. "Remember," she told them, touching her nose to each of theirs in turn. "Stay hidden. Stay safe. And no matter what happens here on deck, do *not* leave this boat."

"We promise," Cosmo said in his tiny voice, while Violet and Jack stared solemnly at the floor.

"I hope to see you again someday," Clara whispered as she walked away.

CHAPTER 18
MUTT

Monday, April 15, 1912
1 AM

Mutt said a quick goodbye to the kittens, then trotted after Clara, glancing back at the lifeboat every so often to make sure the kittens stayed put.

"They will be all right," he told Clara when he'd caught up, hoping with every part of himself that it would be true.

Clara didn't answer. She simply nodded and continued down the deck away from the humans. There seemed to be a definite tilt to the floor beneath Mutt's feet. Several times he felt himself stumble when the ground wasn't quite where he'd expected it to be.

"You're hurt?" he asked, noticing Clara's limp.

"It's nothing," she snapped, not pausing or slowing down, even though she was clearly in pain and her paw was bending at a funny angle. "Which class did you say your human was traveling in?"

"Steerage," Mutt replied. "Third class—although I guess Alice could be anywhere on the ship now."

Clara paused and gave him a grim smile. "Third-class cabins are mostly on the E and D decks toward the stern of the ship," she told him at the top of a flight of stairs. "You'll have to go down at least two floors. Although...I think I might have seen her earlier. There was a girl called Alice with her father."

Mutt felt his heart race with a mixture of excitement and dread. If Clara was right, he could finally be reunited with Alice—once he found her. But that would also mean that Alice was in danger. He couldn't wait a moment longer. He had to find her now.

"Did she have red hair like fire?" he asked.

Clara nodded. "If your girl *is* on this ship, she will most likely be somewhere down there, if she hasn't already made her way up to the boat deck." She paused. "There are gates between the first- and second-class decks and steerage. It might be difficult to find a way back up to the lifeboats."

"Thank you," Mutt said. "I have to try. Will you come with me? We can find my girl and then join the kittens."

Clara shook her head sadly. "A captain never abandons his ship, and a ship's cat never abandons her captain," she said.

"I understand," Mutt said, even though he wished Clara would get into the boat with the kittens and save herself. But he could no more leave Alice than Clara could leave her master. "Thank you for not having me thrown overboard."

Clara nodded. "Thank you for looking after the kittens," she said. She started to walk away but paused to look back. "If you see them again, please make sure they find a good home."

"I will," Mutt promised. His stomach sank at the thought that his promise might be little more than empty words. The chances of any of them getting out of this alive seemed slim at best. But at least the kittens would have a chance on the lifeboat.

"Oh, and, Mutt?" Clara called back. "I don't much

like dogs," she said. "But I don't think I've ever met a finer dog than you."

Mutt opened his mouth to reply, but the ship lurched suddenly and he slid down the deck, narrowly avoiding being hit in the head by a wayward deck chair.

When he had regained his footing, Clara was gone.

"Good luck," he whispered.

Mutt raced down the stairs to the third-class promenade deck, which was already crammed with passengers, many of them wearing life jackets over their night-clothes. He searched the crowds for any sign of Alice or the master, stopping every few seconds to sniff the air for her scent, but there was no sign of either of them.

Mutt decided to search the lower decks, where Clara had told him the third-class cabins for families were, pushing against the ever-increasing flow of humans flooding onto the deck until he found himself in a nearly abandoned corridor. Water had already started seeping into the carpet. Mutt ran down the hallway, which was now definitely at a tilt, racing along the twists and turns, sniffing as he went, his ears pricked up to listen for any clue that Alice might be close by.

He had almost given up hope when he turned another corner, panting and out of breath, and caught the briefest flash of red hair heading toward another stairwell. *Alice!* Mutt ignored the cramps in his legs and the burn in his lungs and raced toward her, barking again and again, feeling as though his heart might explode with joy. The girl was being pulled along by a tall, broad-shouldered man.

"Papa! I hear Mutt," she was saying to him. "Papa!"

But the master was pulling her so hard that she couldn't turn, so Mutt ran up and grabbed the master's heel in his jaws, clamping down hard.

"Argh!" the master yelled, spinning to see what had caught him. His face changed from fear to anger to surprise all in the space of a single breath. "Mutt?" he said. "Is that really you? How on earth...?"

"Mutt!" Alice cried, dropping to her knees with a sob that turned into a fit of giggles as Mutt licked at her face and her hands, his tail wagging so hard it felt as if it might drop off. He rubbed his nose to hers as she laughed and kissed him and cried his name over and over again. "Mutt, Mutt, Mutt. I thought I'd never see you again!" she whispered. She looked up at her father. "How did he get on board the ship?"

The master shook his head, rubbing his eyes as though he couldn't quite believe what was right there in front of him. He opened his mouth to answer as a heavy crash rang out along the corridor. The floor beneath them shifted slightly downward and a door flew open, smashing into the wall. Thousands of pieces of broken crockery and glass came tumbling out into the hallway.

Water ran along the floor, covering their feet and paws. The master grabbed Alice's hand, pulling her away from Mutt. "We need to get to the lifeboats," he said. "Now!"

They ran through the ever-rising water, with Mutt hot on their heels. A single rat swam past Mutt, heading in the opposite direction. For a second, Mutt's breath caught in his throat as he thought it might be King Leon, but then he saw the rat's long pink tail and realized it wasn't. King Leon's words came back to him, though, and he stopped, barking up at Alice and the master, keeping his eyes trained on the rat, not wanting to lose sight of it because the moment he did, he knew they would be lost. Mutt barked again and gripped the hem of Alice's nightdress between his jaws, pulling as hard as he could in the direction of the rat.

"He wants us to follow him!" Alice cried.

"Don't be silly, Alice!" the master shouted. "We need to follow the other passengers. That's not the right way!"

Mutt narrowed his eyes and dug his claws into the floor, pulling harder and more urgently at the sodden hem of Alice's nightdress until it felt as if it was going to rip in two. The rat was almost at the end of the corridor, which meant Mutt would lose sight of him any second. *Follow the rats*, King Leon had told him, and that was exactly what Mutt intended to do. Mutt pulled Alice so hard that she stumbled a few steps forward. He took advantage of the slight momentum and yanked harder, dragging Alice along little by little until she relented and ran after him.

"Come on, Papa!" she shouted. "Mutt is showing us the way."

CHAPTER 19

CLARA

Monday, April 15, 1912
1:30 AM

Clara slipped through the crowd, hurrying away from Mutt as fast as she could manage, struggling to stay upright with the searing pain that burned through her leg. She didn't allow herself to look back. She hoped he would find his human and a way onto one of the lifeboats before it was too late.

"Women and children first!" the officers and crew shouted above the roaring noise of the passengers gathering on the deck. The head baker and his staff passed by, heading toward the lifeboats with their arms full of loaves of bread.

The crew continued to load the boats one by one, calling out directions and swinging them out over the open water to be lowered into the ocean far below. Many of the passengers pushed and fought their way forward, desperate to get a space on a lifeboat. The reluctance to leave the great ship had long passed, replaced with urgency as the humans realized what would happen to them if they stayed behind. Clara hoped the kittens would stay in their own lifeboat and not try to find her. Violet was a sensible kitten, Clara told herself. She would make sure that her brothers did as they were told.

Clara wove through the legs of people lining up along the deck, trying to get into the boats.

"I need to get on a lifeboat!" a woman shouted.

"Me too!" another yelled. "I have two children with me."

"What about the men?" a man yelled. "We deserve a spot, too." A group of men close by roared in agreement at this and started pushing harder against the crowd.

Earlier, the passengers had formed orderly lines at the lifeboats, patiently waiting their turn. But now, as it became glaringly clear that more than half the lifeboats had already been filled and there were still hundreds of humans left on the ship, the crowd was panicked and disorderly.

High above, flares were being launched into the sky in an attempt to get the attention of any boats or ships sailing close by. Red flashes of light streaked out into the darkness, then floated slowly down to be extinguished by the water below. Some of the humans screamed as the boat listed forward, and at the sight of the flares, which made it all too clear just how much danger they were in. Clara jumped to avoid being crushed under the feet of a particularly rowdy group of men who were demanding to be let onto a boat.

Clara hobbled beneath a wooden bench to catch her breath, the pain in her leg almost unbearable, then she forced herself to continue on, desperate to get to the comfort of her captain's arms. As she passed the smoking room, she saw a group of men in full evening dress. They wore black jackets and trousers with white silk cravats and bow ties. They were drinking whiskey and smoking cigars as though they hadn't a care in the world. Clara thought it strange that they weren't panicking like the other passengers, but then she realized that they had accepted their fate—just as she had. There was nothing to be done now. Either help would come in time to rescue them all, or it wouldn't. Neither fear nor anger could change that fact.

The band had gathered near the stern of the ship, close to where the final lifeboats were being loaded, and had started playing a jolly tune in an attempt to keep spirits up, Clara supposed. They, too, had probably decided to play out their roles to the end, and that was what Clara intended to do. She was the captain's cat, and she would not abandon her post now.

Thomas Andrews, the ship's architect, stood a little way away, listening to the music but seeming lost in thought. A steward was trying to get his attention, holding up a white life jacket and urging him to at least put it on, but Andrews waved him away, and after a moment, the steward left him alone. When she reached the wheelhouse, Clara felt her heart swell as she was finally reunited with her captain. He shouted out orders to his officers to continue sending up flares until there were none left, while the wireless operators continued to send out distress calls in the Marconi room, hoping that a ship might be close enough to come to their rescue in time.

"I think I see a boat!" someone called.

"Use the Morse lamp to send out a signal," the captain said. "They must come at once!"

The captain and officers rushed to the deck to send flashing light signals across the water using the Morse lamp, then waited with bated breath. A second later there was a flash of light in reply on the horizon, and Clara felt her hopes soar—maybe salvation was in sight after all.

The captain's man signaled again, the Morse lamp clicking on and off. Again they waited, hoping that the faintest of lights along the horizon was a passing ship.

"Try again!" the captain ordered.

But as they watched, the faint light on the horizon that they had taken for another ship faded, along with their hopes of rescue. If there were any boats around now, they would all be too far away to reach them in time. The captain knew this as well as Clara. He turned to look at each of the remaining officers in turn.

"It's every man for himself now," he told them, officially relieving them of their duty.

The men paused, looking at one another, then back to the captain for some other sign, some other way for them to save the day at the last minute. But there was none. And so, one by one, with a shake of the captain's hand and a brief "Good luck" or "Farewell," they left the bridge, and Clara and her captain were alone.

Clara gave a small meow to let the captain know that she was still there and wouldn't be going anywhere. He picked her up gently and smiled. "Dearest Clara," he said, stroking her head. "It looks as though this will be our final voyage."

Clara meowed again to tell him she understood. The captain kissed her head. Then, still holding her close, he gripped the ship's wheel, taking charge of his ship for the last time.

Monday, April 15, 1912
1:50 AM

Mutt chased after the rat with Alice and the master following, despite the master's protests. The rat moved quickly, skillfully turning left and right without any hesitation, as though he had lived on the ship his entire life. Finally, they reached a narrow stairwell and the rat scurried up the stairs. Mutt found himself out in the open air, back on the boat deck, where large crowds were forming.

"See?" Alice said to her father. "I knew Mutt would lead us the right way."

There was a sudden explosion in the sky above, and

Mutt yelped as the night was filled with a crimson light that turned the faces of the humans bloodred as they all looked up. Three more lights followed in swift succession, and the sight seemed to work the crowd up into a worried frenzy as they pushed forward, all vying for a space on one of the few lifeboats that remained on the deck. At the back of the ship, a group of men worked to untie the two collapsible lifeboats, but as they tried to attach the first one to the strange winchlike contraption that lowered the boats into the sea, it fell, landing with a loud smack upside down on the deck below.

The master glanced down at Mutt, giving him a doubtful look, then turned his attention back to the remaining lifeboats.

"We have to get you onto a boat," the master told Alice, placing his large, callused hand on her back to push her forward.

"There are too many people, Papa!" she cried, clinging to a tuft of Mutt's hair with one hand and her father's arm with the other. "I'm scared."

"It's all right," the master said. "They have to let you on one of the boats—it's women and children first. Go on, now. I'm right behind you."

They continued to push their way through the crowd. It was easier for Alice and Mutt because of their small size, but a few times Mutt turned to see the master jostling and elbowing other men in the crowd to keep up. To their left, a large group of men who appeared to be from third class, judging by their worn clothes and tired, haggard-looking faces, began shouting and arguing with one of the officers, who was telling them to stay back.

"Women and children only!" the officer yelled, but the men paid him no mind, trying to push past and swarm the lifeboat, which was already swinging precariously out over the water. A woman screamed, and before Mutt knew what was happening, an earsplitting gunshot rang out as an officer fired his gun in the air, silencing the crowd.

The master seized his chance and pushed Alice through to the front so that she was standing directly in front of the lifeboat. "I have a child here!" he yelled. "Let this child on the boat."

The officer manning the boat nodded and held out his hand to Alice to help her on board, but she pulled back, shaking her head. "Not without my papa and Mutt," she said.

"Alice," the master urged, pushing her forward. "Go on, now. Me and Mutt will be right behind you, won't we, boy?" he said, glancing down at Mutt.

Mutt looked from the master to Alice and then at the lifeboats. There were two remaining: the one to their left and the one right in front of them. The one on the left was already being lowered into the water. The kittens' boat was no longer on the deck, and Mutt hoped they were still safely hidden under the bench.

Mutt realized this was Alice's only chance. If she didn't get on the boat, she wouldn't get on one at all. He nudged Alice forward with his head, and the officer peered down at him.

"No dogs allowed," the officer said.

"But she has a dog!" Alice cried, pointing to a lady already seated in the lifeboat. She was dressed in a thick brown fur coat that reached to the floor. At first, Mutt couldn't see what Alice was referring to, because the dog was camouflaged against his human's coat, but then Mutt spotted him. It was Fifi, the little yappy dog, shivering in his mistress's arms.

The officer sighed impatiently. "She is a first-class passenger," he told them. "And she insisted."

The lifeboat started to swing away from the boat deck, and Alice spun to bury her face in the master's stomach. "I want to stay with you and Mutt, Papa!" she cried.

"Alice," the master said, his voice cracking. "Please. You have to get on the boat now. It's going to leave without you. *Please, Alice.*"

Mutt watched as the boat moved inch by inch, out and away from the deck. There was no more time to think. He had to make Alice get on the lifeboat. He had to save her. He took Alice's nightdress in his teeth and pulled. The master, seeing what Mutt was doing, nudged Alice toward the officer, giving him a small nod. The officer grabbed Alice beneath the arms and lifted her into the boat just as it moved away.

Alice stood in the boat as it swayed precariously over the water. She shrieked, reaching out for Mutt and the master, but the lifeboat was already being lowered into the water. "Papa!" she screamed. "Mutt!"

A woman sitting on the bench in the lifeboat took Alice's hand, and Alice dropped down beside her, sobbing and crying out for Mutt and the master until Mutt could no longer see the boat. But he could still hear her calling out for them. Mutt whined, laying his ears flat against his head and wishing he could shut out the terrible sound that tore open his heart.

Alice!

Mutt looked back at the master, who wiped away the tears in his eyes with the back of his rough, fisherman's hands. The master whispered, "That was the last boat, Mutt. My little girl is saved, but I'm afraid we are not. That was the last boat."

CHAPTER 21
MUTT

Monday, April 15, 1912
2 AM

The final lifeboat had been lowered into the water, taking Alice and any hope Mutt had of going with her to the New World with it. The deck was now slanting so much that it was almost as if they were back on the hilltop at home, looking out over the Solent. Mutt had to dig his claws deep into the wood to keep from sliding toward the bow, which dipped closer and closer to the water with every passing second.

Passengers still crowded the railings, looking down at the water and trying to find some way onto a lifeboat. Some climbed over the railings and jumped into the sea to try their luck swimming to a lifeboat. One man with a slightly crazed look in his eyes ran along the deck, throwing every single deck chair and loose piece of furniture he could lay his hands on into the water so that those already in the sea might have something to cling to. Many of them probably couldn't see far enough past the crowd to realize that all the lifeboats were gone.

But Mutt knew the truth: All they had left was the smallest of hopes that another boat might come to their rescue before it was too late. Mutt watched Alice's boat row away from the doomed ship for as long as he could to make sure she was safely away. Even above the clamor and chaos of voices around him he could still hear her crying out for him and her father.

Mutt turned and looked up at the master beside him, to see what they would do next, but the master was no longer there. Another man dressed in similar clothes and battered brown boots had taken his place in the mass of humans. The crowd pushed forward, pushing Mutt with them, squeezing him against the edge of the ship until he could barely breathe. He tried to wriggle his way free, but there were too many of them. Too many legs and bodies forming a barrier between him and the master—wherever he was. Mutt took a deep breath and tried to make himself as tall as he could; then he barked and growled at the humans closest to him, baring his teeth and snarling as they glanced down, surprised to see a dog at their feet.

Slowly, slowly, they moved aside, afraid they might be bitten, and Mutt finally broke free. The boat lurched suddenly downward another few inches. Deck chairs and humans alike slid down the promenade and into the freezing water, which had now risen over the bow, moving farther and farther up toward the crowd. Mutt's mind flashed back to when he was a pup, and the absolute terror he had felt at being in the water, almost drowning. His stomach flopped.

Mutt frantically sniffed the air for his master's scent, but his nostrils were overwhelmed with the smell of blood and sweat and fear. Then he remembered the two collapsible lifeboats at the back of the ship. The master had worked on boats all his life, and Mutt thought maybe that was where he had headed. Mutt ran up the ever-increasing incline, along with some humans who had the same idea or were just trying to stay out of the water as long as they possibly could. Below him on the steerage deck, more humans were doing the same, clinging to railings or ropes or anything else they could get their hands on. Some climbed on top of each other's shoulders to reach the higher decks.

The lights flickered, and all went black for a moment. Screams filled the air, and it seemed this was it—the final descent into the big blue. Mutt held his breath.

But the lights flickered on again. Mutt pushed on, passing a group of humans standing before a man dressed in black robes, like the reverend at Alice's church. Their eyes were closed and they knelt on the deck, listening to the man's prayers, even as chaos erupted all around them. Then, just as Mutt passed by, one of the enormous steam funnels gave way, crashing down into the deck with a deafening crack. When Mutt looked back, he could no longer see the group.

The force of the crash seemed to have pushed the ship farther down, and although Mutt could see the back of the ship rising out of the water, he knew he wouldn't make it in time. The deck continued to rise until it was almost vertical. Mutt slid back down, only stopping when his rump landed with a loud thud on the stained-glass window of the humans' gymnasium, which was now horizontal.

Mutt froze, not daring to move in case he lost his footing or the glass gave way beneath his paws. Still, the back of the great ship continued to rise. Out in the big blue, Mutt could see the lifeboats lit by bright lanterns—most of the boats only half full—rowing away from the *Titanic* rather than toward the hundreds of humans who were already in the water.

The lights on the ship flickered once more, and this time, they went out for good. Mutt felt a surge of panic seep into his body as his eyes adjusted to the pitch-black night. He struggled to get his bearings.

Mutt stayed low, crawling across the narrow ledge toward the edge of the ship as the *Titanic* sank, lower and lower, into the churning black water below. A terrible noise like metal being crushed echoed around him, and Mutt whimpered. He dug his nails into the wood, his body freezing in terror, afraid that the ship might disappear beneath him at any moment, to be replaced with nothing but endless water.

There were two choices, Mutt told himself, chancing a quick glance over the edge—go down with the ship, or jump into the water. He didn't much like his odds either way. The surface of the water was covered with debris from the broken ship—chairs and trunks and crates. A single deck chair floated almost directly below, but it was so very far down now. Mutt wasn't sure he could make it without breaking all of his limbs, or worse.

Mutt's thoughts raced through his head. He had to make a decision. He couldn't stay on the ship much longer. As soon as it went down, he would be pulled beneath the surface. He raised his front paws onto the railings. He had to jump. Jump or fall or drown. Not much of a choice, but maybe if he did make it, the lifeboats would come back....

Mutt closed his eyes. He tried not to think of how cold and wet the water would be, or about the fact that he didn't even know whether he could swim. It had seemed simple enough when he'd seen other dogs at the beach do it—casually moving their legs back and forth in the water. But Mutt wasn't like other dogs. Mutt hated water.

Huge splinters started to run across the middle of the deck, crackling like breaking ice on a frozen pond as the weight of the sinking ship became too much to bear. The *Titanic* ripped apart into two halves. As the stern started to fall back toward the water, almost in slow motion, Mutt recalled a prayer that Alice's mother used to make Alice recite every night before she went to bed. He didn't know much about what it was for, or why she did it, but it seemed to bring Alice's mother comfort.

So he took one final, deep breath, hoping it would not be his last.

And he jumped.

CHAPTER 22
CLARA

Monday, April 15, 1912
2:15 AM

The captain held Clara tightly in his arms as the water rose rapidly beneath his feet, lapping against the glass window of the bridge. It wasn't something that he often did when they were at sea—hugging. Usually they each kept to their own duties: the captain at the helm of the ship, and Clara making sure that the animals on board were kept in line, and usually chasing and eating the rats who had sneaked on board. She felt the strangest twinge of regret about wanting to eat Mutt's rat friend.

The frigid water breached the bridge, rushing into its open sides to surround them as the front of the ship dipped farther forward and the stern rose out of the ocean. The water crept to the captain's knees, then up to his waist in a matter of seconds. Clara tried not to focus on it. Or the fact that out on the deck beside them, anything that wasn't held in place slipped into the water. Clara closed her eyes and rubbed her head against the captain's fluffy white beard, breathing in his scent one last time as he hugged her closer to him, whispering that he was with her, that he wouldn't let go, while trying to keep his balance as the floor beneath them moved down, down, down until they were almost vertical. The ship paused for a moment, bobbing like a buoy in the water.

Then it lurched forward, throwing the captain and Clara toward the window, but still he did not lose his grip. The water raged around them, engulfing them as the ship sank farther and farther. As though it were being gobbled up into the dark depths below.

Clara took a deep breath, telling herself to be strong. To be brave. She gave the captain a final, small meow to let him know that she was with him. That she would be by his side until the very end.

Her beloved captain.

And as the water rose up to meet them, the captain gave Clara a kiss on the head and said: "Farewell, old friend."

CHAPTER 23
MUTT

Monday, April 15, 1912
2:17 AM

The air was knocked out of Mutt's lungs as he hit the freezing water. He narrowly missed a human who was grabbing frantically at anything he could get a grip on. Mutt paddled quickly out of his way before the man decided to use *him* as a life preserver. Mutt had been aiming for a deck chair he'd seen floating on the surface but had misjudged his landing. The deck chair had glided out of his reach with the small wave he'd created as he hit the water.

Mutt frantically moved his legs back and forth as fast as he could, managing to keep his head above the water as splashes echoed around him—tens, maybe hundreds of humans following his lead, taking the only option they had left, unless they chose to go down with the ship. It wasn't much of a choice. Mutt thought they were probably all doomed either way, but if he could somehow get to a lifeboat or cling to *something*, he might have the slightest of chances.

His breath came out in fast puffs of white. The faster he tried to paddle, the more he felt himself being weighed down, unable to catch a breath. He spun around, searching for something—anything—to grab hold of before exhaustion dragged him down beneath the waves.

He caught sight of a flash of white in the darkness ahead of him and forced his stiffening limbs to keep paddling. It was one of the life jackets most of the humans were wearing, but this one was abandoned. Or maybe it had slipped off whoever had been wearing it. Either way, Mutt didn't wait for someone else to claim it. He dragged one of his front paws out of the water to grip the jacket with his claws, then the other. It wasn't strong enough to hold his entire weight, but it at least gave him the chance to pause for a moment to catch his breath and decide what to do next.

Just as Mutt finally managed to drag in a deep breath and feel his racing heart calm a little, there was a deafening splash behind him. The force threw him forward. He clung desperately to the jacket, feeling his grip loosen. A hand caught Mutt's tail, pulling him beneath the surface as he tried to hold on to the life jacket in the vain hope that he could somehow keep both of them afloat, but it was futile—he barely had the strength to keep himself up, let alone a human.

Water closed in over his head as Mutt sank beneath the surface. His lungs screamed with the desperate need for air as he kicked his legs wildly. He tried not to take in any water, and at the same time to hold back his terror and the memory of what had happened to him as a pup. Just as he felt himself losing hope, an image of Alice's face flashed before him. He had to fight. He had to get to Alice—he was all she had left. But the man would still not let go, so Mutt did the only thing he could, hoping it might save them both. Mutt turned and sank his teeth deep into the man's hand, yanking it upward in the direction of the surface.

The man immediately released his grip and swam back up to the surface. Mutt kicked his legs hard, trying to follow, but he lost his bearings. All he could see was darkness in every direction, and he could no longer tell whether he was pushing himself up or down or was just swimming around underwater in circles. All he knew was that if he didn't reach the surface soon, he wouldn't make it.

Mutt's vision grew darker, and distant lights danced a little way ahead, like fireflies calling to him to give chase. He didn't know if they were real or not, but he followed the lights with every last ounce of energy in his stiffening limbs until, finally, he broke free.

The noise that greeted him was deafening. Hundreds of voices called out for help, splashing around in the water for something to hold on to. For some kind of rescue or savior that wasn't there. Mutt saw a large leather trunk floating in the water close by, and he paddled over to it, with renewed hope burning in his belly. There might not be any lifeboats nearby, but for a dog, a trunk was just as good.

He dug his claws into the trunk and tried to pull himself up but slipped back into the water. He tried again, this time gripping a strap around the trunk's center with his teeth. His claws scrabbled and scratched against the exposed leather until, finally, he pulled himself up and onto the trunk. He had made it! He was out of the water. He would have howled with joy had it not been for the fact that he was still lost and alone in the middle of the freezing big blue.

A series of small explosions went off in the water behind him as the *Titanic*'s great engines were submerged. Mutt spun to see the great ship standing almost upright in the water, its dark shape a silhouette against the brightness of the stars. The vast propellers that steered the ship rose high in the sky. It seemed to hang there for a moment, and Mutt thought it might not go down after all and would right itself, but as the last funnel collapsed and broke away, crashing down to sink to the seabed, the ship followed. The *Titanic* slipped quietly beneath the surface until it disappeared completely.

It had taken less than three hours from the moment the *Titanic* hit the iceberg to its being lost forever beneath the ocean. And now Mutt, and all those who still had air left in their lungs, had nothing but miles and miles of the big blue to cling to.

CHAPTER 24
MUTT

Monday, April 15, 1912
2:20 AM

Mutt lay on his side atop the leather trunk, his chest heaving as he coughed up water and tried to drag air down into his screaming lungs. The trunk bobbed in the water as small waves lapped against the sides. It would have been an almost-soothing sensation if Mutt hadn't been so numb from cold that he could no longer feel most of his body. That...and the chorus of terrified voices that seemed to echo all around him. Fighting to stay afloat, to stay alive in the icy water.

Mutt searched for any sign of the great ship, but it had gone. Along with all the humans who had remained on board. Who didn't have a choice. Along with his friends, Clara, his master, King Leon. Mutt still held on to the hope that King Leon might have found a way out; if anybody could survive, King Leon could. Mutt trembled as he tried not to think of it. Tried to focus on staying afloat. On breathing. On staying alive.

He couldn't accept that he would never see his girl again. He felt a small spark of fire in his belly, born of his sheer will to stay alive. He had come all this way, faced the very worst of his fears, and he was still here. Somehow, clinging on. He couldn't give up now. He wouldn't. He *would* find his Alice again. She had no one else left now—he was all she had. He couldn't let her live alone for the rest of her life. What would happen to her? Who would look out for her? Protect her?

Mutt forced himself to move his paws and wag his tail to get the blood flowing again through his limbs, even though his sodden fur was so frozen that there were tiny icicles hanging from the ends in silvery beads. When he could feel a slight tingle in his paws, he moved his legs. Then slowly, so slowly so that he wouldn't rock the trunk or submerge it beneath the water, he rolled himself over and onto his belly with shaking legs.

He peered out into the darkness. With the lights of the great ship gone and no moon in the sky, it was hard to make out much more than the shifting dark shapes in the water surrounding him. He tried not to think of what they might be, instead focusing on his sense of smell and hearing, cocking his head to one side to listen intently for any sound that might mean salvation. For any lifeboats that might be close by. He looked for their lamplight but couldn't tell whether the faraway twinkling of lights came from the stars or the boats far in the distance.

There! The smallest of sounds caught his attention, floating above the haunting noises around him. It was only because he had heard the very same sound only yesterday that he recognized it at all. The noise came again, and Mutt pushed himself slowly up onto his haunches, narrowing his blurry eyes to focus in the direction the sound was coming from. As he focused, it seemed to get louder, carried across the water by the slightest of breezes, and this time there was definitely no mistaking it—the high-pitched bark of a small, yappy dog.

Fifi!

Mutt tried to calm himself so that he wouldn't make

any sudden movements and sink his trunk before he had a chance to be saved, but he couldn't contain his hope. The last time he had seen the yappy dog was with his owner, sitting inside a lifeboat as it was being slowly lowered into the water away from the doomed ship. The very same lifeboat that Alice had reluctantly been lifted into!

Mutt barked, but the cold and all the salty water he had swallowed meant that it came out as barely more than a hoarse screech. He tried again, not caring that his throat felt as if he had swallowed a thousand pins.

"I'm here. Alice! I'm here."

He paused for a moment, waiting for a reply or any sign that they might have heard him, but all was quiet. He barked again, and again, and again. But as the seconds turned into minutes, his heart sank and he felt a chill shudder through him that was more than just the cold night air. He rested his head on his paws. He felt his eyelids start to droop and his heart slow. He was so tired.

Just as his eyes closed and the darkness drew in around him, he heard a small bark and a shout. A single word made his eyes fly open and his heart race once again: "Mutt!"

Mutt barked and barked, blinded by the light of an

oil lamp that shone brightly through the gloom. As the lifeboat drifted closer, the light grew bigger and brighter, until Mutt squinted up to see a group of faces peering back at him. He searched among them until he found what he was looking for—Alice! His Alice! She beamed back at him, wiping away tears with the back of her hand as she called his name again and again, clambering over the other humans to reach him. "Mutt! It's really you. Mutt!"

The officer steering the boat set down the oil lamp and reached out to lift Mutt from the trunk, stopping short at the sound of a shrill shriek from the back of the lifeboat.

"It's just a dog!" a woman cried. "We should leave him behind. He'll get us wet and cold and…" She trailed off, glancing at the water, then quickly away again.

Alice turned on the woman, jabbing a finger in the air at Fifi, who was snuggled beneath the woman's fur coat. "You have your dog!" she cried. "Why can't I have mine?"

Mutt saw the look of pure fire burning in Alice's eyes, and her hands clenched into fists. He had seen that look before, and it meant that Alice wouldn't be backing

down. Not now. Not ever. "She has her dog!" Alice yelled at the officer, her eyes red-rimmed. "We can't even save *one* frozen dog?"

Alice dropped down onto the bench, and the woman sitting beside her pulled her into a hug as Alice sobbed into the woman's overcoat, which had been thrown on over her nightdress. "We can't save *one*?" Alice whispered.

The officer reached out and pulled Mutt toward him, rubbing at the frozen droplets around his eyes before passing him over the heads of the other humans to Alice. Alice hugged Mutt tighter than she'd ever held him before, and Mutt licked at her face, his tail wagging even though it was freezing.

He couldn't believe that they had both made it, despite everything—they were here together and they were alive! Mutt thought he would gladly stay in Alice's arms for the rest of his life if it meant they would never be apart again.

Alice kissed Mutt's head, then wrapped a warm blanket around his shoulders, sobbing into his fur, saying "*Mutt*" over and over again until, finally, she fell silent. The officer carefully rowed the lifeboat through the debris and away from the site where the *Titanic* had once been.

Mutt felt his eyelids droop as he and the humans seemed to float aimlessly on the big blue, waiting for someone to rescue them. None of the humans talked about what would happen if nobody came.

"The girl's right," the woman beside Alice said suddenly, startling Mutt awake. "We have plenty of space in this lifeboat. We need to search the water. There might still be survivors out there—we should have returned as soon as the ship was lost." She glared at the officer, a steely look in her eyes. "Take us back."

"No!" shrieked the yappy dog's mistress. "There are too many and there's not enough room on this boat. They would sink us all!"

"This boat isn't even half full!" the woman replied, pointing to the empty benches. "If we can save one more life," she added, "just one—then we should."

Alice stroked Mutt's head and nodded as the women argued back and forth.

Then Mutt heard a faint sound on the wind. His ears pricked up as he strained to listen beyond the woman's incessant shrieking and her yappy dog.

"Shut up!" Mutt barked at the dog.

Fifi scowled at Mutt. "You should be thanking me!" he yapped. "I saved your life."

"You?" Mutt growled. "How did *you* save my life?"

"I could smell you," Fifi replied. "I knew you were close, so I barked to get my owner's attention."

"Well," Mutt growled, quieter this time. "Thank you...I suppose."

"You suppose?" the yappy dog squeaked.

Mutt was about to argue some more, but the noise came again. "Be quiet!" Mutt and Alice snapped at the same time, and both Fifi and his owner finally shut up.

Mutt scanned the water, looking for the source of the noise. A little way ahead, he could see the faint outline of something large rising up and out of the water. It was too large to be a dolphin—Mutt had seen them visit the beach back home—but it was too small to be a whale. A sudden thought jogged his memory as he realized what he was looking at—it was one of the collapsible lifeboats, but it was upside down.

The sound came again. Barely more than the tiny shred of hope he had left within him, but it was there. Mutt hoped with all his heart that the sound wasn't just a figment of his imagination grown from the sliver of hope. He jumped down from Alice's lap and barked. His throat was still hoarse, but he leaped up and over the other survivors to the front of the lifeboat and placed his paws on the bow, barking in the direction of the collapsible. The lady was right, he thought—if they could save just one more life, they should.

The officer changed course at the insistence of Alice and some of the other humans, raising the oil lamp to search for any signs of movement in the gloom. The collapsible had somehow flipped in the water, but there were still humans clinging to it. There were almost ten men, maybe more, sitting on top of the boat. As they rowed closer, though, the hope in Mutt's heart faded. The humans looked like icicles themselves. Their hands and lips were blue.

Then, slowly, one by one as they saw what was in front of them, saw that salvation had arrived, the men moved their freezing limbs to face the lifeboat. Their frozen mouths spread into smiles as they hugged one another.

"We are saved!" they shouted in shivering voices. "We are saved!"

The officer and another passenger still dressed in his pajamas helped the men climb into the lifeboat, handing them blankets as the others made room. One of the men who had been in the water the entire time, clinging to the collapsible, and was miraculously still alive, gave Mutt a grin as he dripped into the boat and over Fifi's mistress's head, much to her annoyance.

Mutt watched Alice scan the faces of the men as they boarded, desperately hoping that one of them might be the master. But as she shook her head at each one in turn, she looked to the collapsible. There was only one man left, and he lay still on the very end of the boat, his face turned away.

The officer hailed the man a few times, but he did not move or return the call.

"It's too late," the officer said quietly, looking back at the other passengers. "I'm sorry."

He set the lantern down beside Mutt and turned to pick up the oars.

Mutt couldn't take his eyes off the man on the boat. Something about him was familiar. Something…He jumped up as he saw the slightest movement. The man lifted his head slowly away from the boat and turned to look at Mutt, his lips trembling as he tried to form the words. He stared right at Mutt, and his eyes widened as though he could hardly believe what he was seeing. Mutt's tail wagged as he barked as loudly as he could to make the officer stop. To see what he had.

"Mutt, what is it?" Alice said, climbing back over the other humans to get to Mutt.

The man in the water finally managed to form a single, stammered word. Not much more than a whisper: *"A-A-Alice!"*

"Papa!" Alice shouted as Mutt joined in, barking along with her. "It's my papa! He's alive!"

CHAPTER 25
MUTT

Monday, April 15, 1912
4 AM

A shower of shooting stars streaked across the endless black sky. The cries had long since died out, but the silence was worse than those awful sounds, because at least while the voices had called out, there had still been hope. The deafening silence meant that all hope was lost—at least, for those who had never had the chance to make it onto one of the lifeboats. Mutt couldn't understand it. He might be an animal whose ways were different from those of the humans, but it still made no sense. Why hadn't they saved more people? Why hadn't they gone back for more?

The answer, he realized as he thought about Fifi's

human's words, was fear. The terrible fear that if they took on more humans their boat might be swamped and flooded and they, too, would be as helpless as those poor souls now floating as silent as stone on the surface of the big blue—although now Mutt could see it as nothing but a black emptiness that surrounded them. Closing in, as they waited. And waited.

There was nothing to do but wait. In the cold, dark morning, wet and freezing, until someone came to their rescue. A man sitting opposite Mutt pulled something from his pocket and extended it to Alice, who hadn't stopped shaking since they had found the master.

"This will do you good," the man said kindly, handing Alice an orange.

The master smiled at the man gratefully and tore the orange open, handing the other half back.

The man shook his head. "You and the girl share it," he said, smiling as Alice sucked at the fruit's sweet juice and a bit of color returned to her cheeks.

"Thank you," the master said, holding his hand down to Mutt to let him lick the juice from his fingers.

The man gave a small laugh. "It's funny," he said. "When I knew we were sinking, that's all I took with me—a handful of oranges. I could have taken my money, jewelry, everything else that I had that can't so easily be replaced. But at that moment, the only thing that entered my mind was that we would need sustenance to survive the night."

The master nodded and pulled Alice close to him. Mutt knew what the man meant. In the end, few *things* truly mattered.

After they had pulled the master on board, their boat had floated aimlessly somewhere in the middle of the big blue. There had been the terrible sounds of bumps and scrapes against the sides of the lifeboat. Some of them were made by the luxurious things from the *Titanic*— furniture, deck chairs, luggage. Mutt had even spotted a crate filled with apples bobbing on the water's surface. Some of them were made by things Mutt couldn't bring himself to think about.

Alice, too, was silent now. The master, swaddled in blankets and a fur coat that another passenger had offered to him, had pulled her into a hug, and she'd drifted off to sleep. Every so often, Mutt could hear the master whisper to Alice: "We made it, Alice. Everything's going to be all right now. We made it."

The relief they all felt was overwhelming, accompanied by guilt—that they had survived when so many others hadn't.

Mutt nudged Alice's legs with his head every so often to make sure she hadn't succumbed to the freezing temperatures of the night. He huddled beneath the bench, tangled up in the hem of Alice's nightdress and blanket. But there was no warmth to be found. No matter how close he got, Mutt could not stop the shivering, shaking feeling that seemed to come from somewhere deep inside and wouldn't let go.

The lifeboats that were closest to one another had been tethered together, but despite the number of survivors on each boat, it was eerily quiet. Mutt thought of the kittens, hoping they had stayed hidden inside the lifeboat. Hoping they were warm and safe. The thought of losing them, too, was almost unbearable. He briefly considered barking to see if they might hear, but then thought better of it. He didn't want them coming out of their hiding place to be discovered by the humans.

The sun had not yet started to rise. One of the men on the boat had thought he'd spotted it rising in the distance, but it had been something the officer called the northern lights. Appearing like a mirage to give them false hope.

And then, finally, it did come—salvation. In the form of another ship, called the *Carpathia*. Not as big as the *Titanic* but big enough to easily accommodate a few hundred extra passengers. But although rescue was so close, the humans didn't have much energy or will left in them to row, instead waiting for the *Carpathia* to draw near and haul them one by one onto the deck, where warm blankets and hot drinks waited for the humans.

Mutt and Alice were unable to climb the rope ladder that had been let down over the side of the *Carpathia*. To Mutt's mild amusement, they had tied a rope to a mail sack, and he and Alice had clambered inside to be hauled up to the ship's deck. As the sack swayed perilously above the waves lapping against the *Carpathia*'s side, Mutt was surprised to find that his fear of water had gone—he had fought a fierce battle against the big blue and survived. Though now that he had survived two close calls with the water, once they were back on dry land he thought he would probably never voluntarily set one paw near the big blue again.

Mutt and Alice were given warm blankets. They sat

on a bench on the deck together in silence, watching the sun rise slowly above the horizon.

Thursday, April 18, 1912

Mutt and Alice sat on the deck, looking out over the water at the lights in the distance. The New World. They were nearly there. The captain and crew of the *Carpathia* had given them everything they needed over the last few days as they'd continued their journey. Food, shelter. Mutt was even allowed to go wherever he pleased, unlike on the *Titanic*, and apart from a few raised eyebrows and disapproving looks at his bedraggled appearance, there had been no threats of his being thrown overboard. Not even when he'd chewed the master's new slippers.

"Mutt!"

A small voice called out across the deck. Mutt leaped down from the bench and ran. He would recognize that voice anywhere. Alice called after him, but he raced on, almost colliding with three small bundles of fur. They pounced onto Mutt's back, covering him with tiny kitten kisses.

"It's you, it's really you!" Cosmo laughed.

"We thought you were lost," Violet sobbed as the three kittens huddled against Mutt's side, purring uncontrollably.

"I searched for you everywhere," Mutt said. "Where have you been?"

Mutt's tail wagged back and forth as he licked the kittens' heads—despite Violet's squealed protests. Then he smiled at the warm, vibrating feeling that spread through his body as the kittens snuggled up to him and purred. He'd never been so happy to see a cat—or three—in his entire life.

"We were in a cabin," Jack said with a sly smile. "But we managed to escape!"

"We were hungry," Cosmo added.

Mutt laughed, thinking that some things never changed.

"I'm so glad you're safe!" he barked.

Since he'd last seen them, he'd had a terrible niggling feeling at the back of his brain that they might somehow not have made it. But they had! They were right here with him, and safe. Never again would he consider cats his enemy. These three kittens were the closest he had ever come to having pups of his own (even though he knew they weren't actually pups).

Cosmo pulled away and looked around, sniffing at the air. "Is Miss Clara with you?" he asked.

Jack nodded. "Or King Leon? Did he make it?"

Mutt forced down the lump in his throat and looked away for a moment as he shook his head. How could he tell them that Clara and King Leon were gone? And what would happen to the kittens now? He had made Clara a promise, but how could he possibly keep that promise when he wasn't sure he even had a home with the master and Alice anymore? He opened his mouth, trying to find the right words, but he didn't need to.

"They're gone, aren't they?" Violet whispered, her bright eyes glistening.

"I don't know what happened to King Leon," Mutt said. "But Clara was so very brave. You—*we*—wouldn't be here now if it weren't for her."

"What will happen to us?" Cosmo sniffled, snuggling close to Mutt.

"We'll find you a human," Mutt said. "Someone good and kind who will love you and take care of you."

Violet peered up at Mutt. "I think we might have found one already," she said.

As she mewed, a little girl no older than Alice rushed

across the deck toward them, pausing for a moment as she saw Mutt. He could tell she was a first-class passenger from the way she wore her hair curled and tied into bright blue ribbons, and because the dress she wore wasn't patched or stained like Alice's.

"There you are!" the girl sang, pulling Jack into a gentle hug. "I've been searching everywhere for you three."

She looked at Mutt and patted him on the head. "Have you found a new friend?" she asked the kittens.

Violet smiled at Mutt and meowed in reply.

The girl frowned. "I'm not sure Mother will let me take a dog home with us," she said slowly.

"You can't have him!" Alice puffed as she finally caught up with Mutt. "He's my dog."

"Oh," the girl said. "That's good. I was worried he had nowhere to go." She gestured to the kittens. "Are these yours, too?" she asked quietly, biting her lip. "Only, only, I found them on the lifeboat and they seemed so lost and scared and Mother said we could keep them because they made everything seem a little less terrible for a moment, and—"

Alice softened and forced a smile at the girl. "It sounds like you'll give them a very good home," she said.

The girl beamed, then called down to the kittens, "Let's go and tell Mother the good news."

Mutt bowed his head in farewell, and one by one, the kittens rubbed their own heads against his. He knew they would likely never see one another again once they reached shore, but he was glad that the kittens would be safe, just as Clara had wanted.

"Goodbye, Mutt," Cosmo called back as they trotted after their human.

"Like Miss Clara said," Jack added with a grin. "You're not so bad...for a dog."

"I'll miss you," Violet said with a sigh before following her brothers.

I'll miss you, too, Mutt thought as he watched them leave.

"We should go, too," Alice said, placing her hand on his head. "Time to meet the New World."

The ship's whistles sounded, and Mutt and Alice gazed out over the big blue as they sailed past a huge statue of a lady holding up a torch to the sky. The bright light from her lamp shone out over the water into the darkness, like a beacon calling them home. The ship docked, and

they found the master and lined up with the other third-class humans. They shuffled along the walkway, back onto the safety of solid land. Despite everything, Mutt couldn't believe he had made it! He was alive, the kittens were safe, and he was with his girl and his master. Mutt couldn't help but feel a surge of hope in his heart, and a bud of excitement in his belly for what the future might hold for them in the New World.

A man wearing a uniform similar to that of the crew on the *Titanic* made a note of the survivors' names, one by one, as they disembarked. Finally, Alice and the master reached the front of the line. This time, though, Mutt didn't have to hide or find a way to sneak around the man. Mutt was with his Alice. Nothing could hurt him now.

"Names?" the man asked.

The master gave their names and the man scribbled them down, then he glanced at Mutt and paused. "This is your dog?" he asked.

Alice nodded and placed her hand protectively on Mutt's head, drawing him closer to her. "His name is Mutt," she told the man, nodding at his clipboard.

But the man didn't write down Mutt's name.

"He was on the ship with you?" he asked, frowning. "On the *Titanic*?"

Alice nodded again. "He found us, he followed us all the way to the ship, and then he—"

The master cut Alice off before she could say any more, and Mutt started to grow uneasy.

"He was with us on the ship and he stays with us now," the master said firmly, looking back at Mutt with a determined expression.

"Sir, I know you have been through a terrible ordeal, but here in the United States of America, we have strict immigration laws," the man told the master. "Any animals coming in from foreign countries must go through quarantine and have the correct paperwork, and—"

"But what about that one?" Alice cried as farther down the quayside, Fifi and his mistress strolled past.

"That one is different, miss," the man said.

"How?" Alice asked loudly, attracting the attention of the humans around them.

The master placed a hand on Alice's shoulder. "Because they are first-class passengers, Alice," he said. The master stared down at Mutt, then turned back to the man. "Sir," he said. "I know that you have rules that you have to follow, and I know you are only doing your job...but...this dog saved my daughter's life. And mine. If it weren't for him, we would both be lost at sea with the countless other poor souls."

The master reached down to pat Mutt on the head, and although he wouldn't be able to tell because he was a human, Mutt smiled back up at him.

"He is the very best of dogs," the master told the man. "And my daughter and I are going nowhere without him."

The man considered Mutt for a moment as more humans gathered around them, having heard the master's plea.

"Let them keep their dog!" a man called out from somewhere in the group.

Mutt looked over, and his heart soared. It was the kind man from the mailroom. Billy! He caught Mutt's eye and winked. Mutt barked back at him in greeting, his tail wagging.

"Yes! Let them keep their dog—haven't they been through enough?" other humans called out. Some of the voices came from passengers of the *Carpathia*, others were fellow *Titanic* survivors. At one point, Mutt thought he saw the *Carpathia*'s captain adding his voice to the rising protest.

"All right, all right!" the man said, relenting. "But you still need paperwork." He pointed the master toward an office at the edge of the quayside, then let them pass to walk down the gangplank with a small cheer from the crowd as they went.

The master ruffled the fur on Mutt's head and gave him a grin. "Good dog, Mutt," he said. "Good dog."

EPILOGUE

Mutt sat at the window of their new home in the New World, keeping the master company. It had been almost a month since they'd arrived in New York. Not on the *Titanic* with the grand fanfare they had been expecting from humans eager to catch a glimpse of the now-infamous ship, but on the *Carpathia*.

The reception had still been chaotic—newspaper reporters had surrounded the survivors, desperate for a quote for the front-page story they were all running with one question at the forefront of everyone's minds—*How could this have happened?* It was a question Mutt had asked himself every day since, and one he would likely ask for the rest of his life. That, and why *he* had been saved when so many others had perished.

Each night, the three of them would sit by the hearth, the master and Alice talking about their day and all the wonderful things they had discovered in the New World, Alice singing songs and the master telling them stories as Mutt lay by their feet. While Alice slept, the master and Mutt remained together in a comfortable silence, the master patting Mutt's head every so often as though checking to be sure he was still there, and telling him he was a good dog.

The silent companions gazed out the window at the stars, until they dozed off into a restless slumber. Often, Mutt found that he would forget about the *Titanic* for the briefest of moments and would wake with a sudden jolt, his heart racing with the sense that he had to find someone—had to save them—before remembering all over again, the knowledge crashing into him with the force of a thousand icy waves.

He had survived.

In the days that followed the sinking of the so-called unsinkable ship, Mutt learned that more than fifteen hundred people had gone down that night with the *Titanic*. Many animals were also lost, but most of those would not be counted or missed by the humans.

Only a lucky few like Mutt, and the kittens, survived

to grieve for those who would likely not be otherwise mourned or remembered. Like brave Clara, the captain's cat: the noblest (and fiercest) animal Mutt had ever met. And King Leon, the rat, who had changed Mutt's mind and heart as to what friendship was. Mutt knew now that even a stinking rat and a scruffy dog could be the best of friends. Mutt still held on to the smallest bud of hope that King Leon might somehow have made it and was back with his family on the streets of Brooklyn.

As he gazed up at the sky, Mutt would imagine that somewhere far, far away among the stars, his lost friends were looking back upon him. He made a silent promise that he would never forget those brave souls—animal or human—who had been lost on that fateful night in April.

Author's Note

The *Titanic* sank more than one hundred years ago, but people remain fascinated by the story of what took place on that fateful night. Books about what actually happened on April 14, 1912, are still being written; movies, television shows, and documentaries are still being made. There are so many extraordinary tales of heartbreak and courage and bravery from that terrible night, along with many unanswered questions. Most significantly: Why did the so-called unsinkable ship sink?

The ship had sixteen watertight compartments with doors that could be opened or closed remotely from the bridge. Even if four of the compartments were damaged, the *Titanic* would remain stable.

When the iceberg was spotted, it was too late to miss it completely, so the quartermaster turned the ship hard left so as not to hit the iceberg head-on. Instead, the hull of the ship scraped along the iceberg. The thing about icebergs, as Clara notes in the story, however, is that often what you see above the surface is only the tip. What lies beneath is much larger. The iceberg ripped long gashes across six of the compartments, dooming the ship.

The immense strength of the ship meant that if they *had* actually hit the iceberg head-on, the *Titanic* likely would not have sunk. But as soon as those six compartments were breached, the water rushed in, rising up and over into each compartment, until the entire hull was flooded.

There are many theories about why the crew didn't spot the iceberg sooner. During the day of the sinking, the Marconi operators received messages from passing ships about icebergs being spotted along the course they were traveling, so the lookouts knew to be cautious.

Some people believe that the lookouts didn't spot the iceberg until it was too late because there were no binoculars on board. Others, that large objects such as icebergs would be much easier to spot with the naked eye, so binoculars would have made little difference. Another theory suggests that an optical illusion on the horizon hid the iceberg until the ship was almost on top of it.

Throughout history, wherever there have been humans, there have been animals. Along with the hundreds of humans who perished that night, there were also animals on board—beloved pets belonging to the passengers, livestock being sold or taken to a new country, where their owners hoped to begin a new life. It is difficult to know precisely how many animals there were on the *Titanic*, as there are no definitive records, but three dogs are recorded to have survived the sinking: two Pomeranians and a Pekingese owned by first-class passengers. One passenger, Ann Elizabeth Isham, reportedly refused to leave the sinking ship, as her beloved Great Dane was too big for the lifeboats.

So I decided to look at the story not from the viewpoint of a human but of an ordinary, slightly rough-and-ready mongrel who cared more about his girl than anything else in the world, and to what lengths he would go to stay with her; a loyal captain's cat who put her duty toward the passengers and her master before her own life; and a stowaway rat. (Rats usually get a raw deal in stories, often being seen as dirty or unpleasant animals, and I wanted to show a different side of them.)

Mutt, Clara, King Leon, and the kittens are fictional characters. None of them were actually on the *Titanic*, and I have taken some liberties with certain elements of the story. For example, Captain Smith did not have a cat, though he did have a dog—an Irish wolfhound that did not accompany him on the voyage. I have Mutt describe colors, when dogs are said to have limited color vision. And when Mutt, Clara, and the kittens hide out in the cargo area, the doors would have been closed for security, but they needed a way to get in and out easily, so in the story this room remains open. But with the larger historical details, such as the timeline of the sinking and the description of the ship's layout, I have tried to be as accurate as possible.

Some of the humans mentioned—Captain Smith, Thomas Andrews, and J. Bruce Ismay—*were* on the ship. But characters such as Alice and her father, Fifi's mistress, and Billy, the kind mailman, are all fictional. Although that is not to say that there weren't people on the *Titanic* who had similar experiences.

There were approximately 2,222 people on board, yet there were only 20 lifeboats that could accommodate a maximum of 1,178 passengers. Many of the lifeboats were released quickly for fear of the deck being flooded with people. One lifeboat had only 12 people on board, and altogether, only 705 people survived. Sadly, many more third-class passengers died than first class, because there were gates separating the third class from the lifeboats on the upper deck. And even if they had reached them, there was not enough room for every passenger.

After the tragedy, an inquiry was set up in the United Kingdom and the United States to find out what had gone wrong, to make sure that it never happened again. As a result of the inquiries, changes were made to ensure that such a tragedy could never occur again. Most important, that ships must have enough lifeboats to accommodate the passengers on board, and the crew should be properly trained on how to deploy them.

Marconi operators were to be stationed at the radio twenty-four hours a day. Improved watertight decks were added to stop any flood from rising further, and speed was to be reduced in foggy and icy conditions.

Had these measures been in place on the doomed *Titanic*, many more, if not *all*, of the passengers and crew of the *Titanic* might have been saved.

SURVIVAL TAILS

THE TITANIC

FACT FILE

Timeline

Wednesday, April 10, 1912

9:30 AM: Passengers arrive to board the *Titanic* in Southampton, UK.

Noon: The *Titanic* sets sail on her maiden voyage across the Atlantic to New York.

6:30 PM: The *Titanic* reaches Cherbourg, France, to pick up and drop off a few passengers and more mail.

Thursday, April 11, 1912

11:30 AM: The *Titanic* reaches Queenstown, Ireland, for more passengers and mail, then continues on toward New York.

Friday, April 12, to Saturday, April 13, 1912

The *Titanic* continues the journey across calm waters.

Sunday, April 14, 1912

Morning: Captain Smith cancels a lifeboat drill for reasons unknown, and takes part in the Sunday church service.

11:39 PM: Lookout Frederick Fleet spots an iceberg in the distance. From the crow's nest, he uses the telephone to alert the officers at the bridge.

On the bridge, the officers signal to the engine room to stop the engines, and they turn the ship's wheel hard port to try to avoid the iceberg.

11:40 PM: The *Titanic* scrapes along the iceberg on the starboard side, ripping a gash in the ship's hull. Water has already begun to pour in.

11:55 PM: Workers prepare lifeboats to evacuate passengers.

Monday, April 15, 1912

Midnight: Water continues to flood the lower decks, and the ship begins listing downward as the compartments fill with water.

12:15 AM: The lifeboats are being swung out, ready to load passengers. Women and children only are called to the lifeboats first.

12:25 AM: Thomas Andrews, the ship's architect, has inspected the damage. Six compartments have been breached. He informs Captain Smith that they have less than two hours before the ship is lost. The Marconi operators begin sending out distress calls to any ships nearby.

12:40 AM: The *Carpathia* receives the distress signal and sets off immediately to the *Titanic*'s aid, but the ship is hours away.

12:45 AM: The lifeboats are being lowered into the water, many only half full, as the officers send out flares and use the Morse lamp to try to get the attention of what they believe could be the *Californian*, a nearby ship.

1:00 AM: The band has assembled on the boat deck and is playing jolly tunes to keep the passengers' spirits up.

1:45 AM: The lifeboats continue to be lowered into the water. The bow of the *Titanic* drops farther into the ocean, with the propellers now hanging out of the water at the stern.

2:05 AM: The sea begins lapping over the deck of the *Titanic*. The last lifeboat has been lowered. The great ship begins to break up.

2:15 AM: The lights go out for good. The stern of the *Titanic* raises up to the sky, then falls back down to the ocean as it splits into two.

2:20 AM: As the bow is dragged underwater, it pulls the rest of the ship down with it, until it disappears beneath the waves. The survivors must now wait for someone to come to their rescue.

3:30 AM: Flares from the *Carpathia* are spotted by survivors in the lifeboats.

4:10 AM: The *Carpathia* reaches the first lifeboats and starts bringing people onto the ship.

8:50 AM: All passengers on the lifeboats have been recovered and the *Carpathia* sets sail for New York.

Thursday, April 18, 1912

9:00 PM: The *Carpathia* arrives in New York.

A Ship of Luxury

The *Titanic* was one of three Olympic-class ocean liners owned by the White Star Line. Along with her sister ships—the *Olympic* built in 1911, and the *Britannic* built in 1914—the ships were intended to be the largest and most luxurious ships the world had ever seen. There was no expense spared and even the third-class accommodations were said to be the equivalent of second class on most other ships. Still, there were only two bathtubs, one for men and one for women, for the entire third-class population, and only families had their own rooms. There were shared bunks in separate quarters for single men and women. The first-class rooms ranged from single rooms to suites with their own private promenades, and were decorated extravagantly with wooden furniture and paneling.

The *Titanic* was made up of ten decks:

BOAT DECK—The uppermost deck where the lifeboats could be found, along with the first-class promenade, gymnasium, bridge, and wheelhouse, and the captain's and officers' quarters. To the rear of these was the Marconi room, where operators used wireless radio to contact other ships and people on shore when they were close enough to land. The radio operators were also given messages by the passengers to send out to friends, family, and business associates on land. When the *Titanic* began sinking, they used Morse code and tapped out the distress signal commonly used at the time—CQD—but as time passed, they used SOS instead. After the sinking of the *Titanic*, the code became commonly used, replacing CQD.

A DECK—This deck had the most luxurious first-class rooms and suites, the first-class lounge, ladies' reading and writing room, and the first-class smoking room.

B DECK—This deck had most of the first-class accommodations, a restaurant, and the popular Café Parisien, which was decorated with lots of wicker furniture and plants. At the stern of this deck was the second-class smoking room.

C DECK—The C deck had more first- and second-class accommodations, as well as the second-class lounge, library, and promenade. And to the stern, the third-class promenade and smoking room.

D DECK—At the bow of this deck was the third-class bar, some more first-class staterooms, a reception room, and a restaurant. To the stern were the hospital and infirmary, and the second-class bar and dining saloon, with second-class accommodations at the very back of the deck and a few third class.

E DECK—This deck had a mixture of staff accommodations, along with first-, second-, and third-class rooms, although there were separate entrances for each. Running right through the center was Scotland Road, which stretched nearly from end to end of this deck, allowing staff to get where they were needed quickly. Elevators also operated from this deck upward to make it easy for the stewards to take trolleys of food, linens, etc., to the first-class passengers on other decks. First class had their own elevators.

F DECK—At the front of this deck were squash courts and the Turkish baths. The heated swimming pool was only the second to have been built on a ship (the first being on her sister ship the *Olympic*). There was also a third-class dining saloon and more accommodations.

G DECK—The front part of the G deck housed the first-class baggage area, the post office, and a racket court. The majority of this deck was taken up with the boiler rooms, coal bunkers, and engines, which reached down to the lowermost deck—the tank top. To the stern were most of the food preparation areas, along with more third-class rooms.

ORLOP DECK—The orlop deck stored refrigerated goods, and was where the mailroom was located directly beneath the post office on the deck above so that the mailmen could easily access all the parcels and letters waiting to be sorted on the journey to and from New York. There were also large storage areas at the bow for other cargo, including motorcars and livestock.

TANK TOP—The tank top was where the engine connected to the propellers.

Animals on the *Titanic*

- There were at least twelve dogs on board the ship, most of whom belonged to first-class passengers and had their own ticket to travel. The dogs stayed in kennels on the F deck and were looked after by the ship's carpenter. (They were walked daily on the poop deck!)

- Chickens were kept in the cargo area. One of the passengers complained about being awoken every morning by a crowing rooster in the hold.

- A canary joined the cargo at Southampton and was dropped off with its owner in Cherbourg.

- There was a ship's cat called Jenny on board. Jenny's job was to keep the ship free from rats and mice, and she slept in one of the galleys. She is said to have joined the ship at Belfast, Ireland, where the *Titanic* was built, after leaving her sister ship, the *Olympic*. While on board, she gave birth to a litter of kittens. When they reached Southampton, Jenny was seen leaving the ship with her kittens. One of the stokers, Jim Mulholland, saw this as a bad omen and decided to leave the ship at Southampton, too. Mulholland later credited Jenny with saving his life.

- A large Newfoundland dog named Rigel was said to have swum in the icy water for hours, barking to guide the *Carpathia* to the lifeboats when it arrived on the scene and saving hundreds of lives. But this turned out to be a hoax.

- A small pig was spotted on board; however, it turned out to be a very realistic-looking mechanical pig that belonged to Edith Rosenbaum Russell, who survived the sinking.

Animal Facts

DOGS

- A dog's sense of smell is at least ten thousand times stronger than a human's.

- Dalmatian puppies are born completely white, and their black spots slowly develop as they grow.

- Dogs can be taught to learn words, commands, and tricks and are roughly as smart as an average two-year-old human. They can also help to detect when a human is ill and are even able to sense when humans with diabetes or epilepsy are getting sick and can alert them.

- Dogs and humans have been allies since at least as far back as the Ice Age, when humans used wolves to help them hunt for food.

- The largest dog breed in the world is the Great Dane. They can grow up to forty-four inches tall.

CATS

- When kittens are born, they are blind for almost two weeks, so they stay close to their mother and siblings.

- Cats have excellent balance. They are great at jumping, and if they fall, they will almost always land on their feet.

- Cats love to sleep and will snooze on average for up to sixteen hours a day.

- They have a great sense of hearing, smell, and vision. They are able to see at night even in almost pitch darkness.

- Cats need to be fast on their feet to catch their prey. They can run up to thirty miles per hour.

RATS

- Rats have a good memory and are very smart. They can even learn tricks.

- They are good swimmers (although they prefer to stay on land), and their long tails mean that they have great balance and are excellent climbers.

- Rats rely on their whiskers to help them find their way around, as their eyesight isn't so great.

- The average rat can grow to between seven and nine inches long, but some can grow up to twenty inches.

- Despite what many people believe, rats are very clean and friendly animals. They don't like to be alone. If one rat in a group is sick or injured, the others will take care of it.

Glossary

BOILER ROOM: the place where the coal was loaded into the furnaces

BOW: the front part of a ship

BRIDGE: the room from which a ship is commanded

BUNKER: where the coal was stored

COLLAPSIBLE: a folding lifeboat, made from canvas

DOCKER: a person who worked at the quayside, loading and unloading cargo

FIREMEN: men who loaded coal into the bunkers to fuel the engines

FURNACE: a heating device that burned the coal to produce steam to run the ship

GALLEY: the kitchen on a ship

GANGPLANK: a narrow walkway from the dock to a ship

HULL: the lowermost, watertight part of a ship

LUGGER: a small sailing ship

OODLE: a stew made from carrots, onions, gravy, and the unwanted cutoffs of meat

PORT: the left-hand side of a ship (when looking toward the bow of the ship)

PORTHOLE: a small round window in a ship

PROMENADE: an area along a deck where passengers can take a stroll

QUARTERMASTER: the officer on a ship responsible for steering

QUAY: the dock running alongside the water to load and unload people and cargo onto ships

QUAYSIDE: the quay and the area around it

SCARPER: to run away

SOLENT: the body of water separating the Isle of Wight from mainland England

STARBOARD: the right-hand side of a ship (when looking toward the bow of the ship)

STEAMER: a ship powered by steam

STEERAGE: the part of the ship providing the cheapest accommodations

STERN: the back part of a ship

STOWAWAY: someone who has sneaked on board a ship without a ticket

STRAIT: a narrow passage of water

WHEELHOUSE: the location of the ship's wheel

WIRELESS: a radio system without wires that allowed ships to communicate with people on shore or nearby boats

Further Reading

BOOKS

Ballard, Robert D. *Exploring the Titanic*. London: Hamlyn Young Books, 1988.

Brewster, Hugh, and Marschall, Ken. *Inside the Titanic*. New York: Little, Brown, 1998.

Chrisp, Peter. *Explore Titanic*. New York: Barron's Educational Series, 2011.

DK Eyewitness: Titanic. New York: DK Children, 2014.

Mayo, Jonathan. *Titanic Minute by Minute*. London: Short Books, 2016.

Stewart, Melissa. *National Geographic Kids Titanic*. Washington, DC: National Geographic Kids, 2012.

WEBSITES

bbc.co.uk/archive/titanic (This features recordings of some of the survivors telling their stories.)

bbc.co.uk/history/titanic

diaperheritage.com (This site has information about the floating bridge that Mutt took to cross over the Solent.)

encyclopedia-titanica.org

nationalarchives.gov.uk/education/resources/life-aboard -titanic

titanicfacts.net

ultimatetitanic.com

DOCUMENTARY

James Cameron's *Ghosts of the Abyss* (2003). (This documentary shows footage taken of the *Titanic* wreckage.)

Scott Palmieri

Katrina Charman lives in a small village in the middle of Southeast England with her husband and three daughters. Katrina has wanted to be a children's writer ever since she was eleven, when her schoolteacher set her class the task of writing an epilogue to Roald Dahl's *Matilda*. Her teacher thought her writing was good enough to send to Roald Dahl himself. Sadly, she never got a reply, but the experience ignited her love of reading and writing. She invites you to visit her online at katrinacharman.com.